MW01076025

A NOTE TO THE READER

This novel includes a soundtrack. Every time (and that means *every* time) you see this lightning bolt ⚡, you can look up the song at the back of the book. You can stop reading, listen to the track, and then go back to reading. Or you can listen to the track while you continue to read. Or you can ignore all the lightning bolts and listen to the songs whenever you feel like it. The Author's intention is to place you inside the moment/scene/character's head. You might already own these songs or you might consider purchasing the tracks. Alternatively, you can follow along with "Ronnie's Playlist" on this novel's YouTube channel. The Author strongly suggests you listen to the tracks with headphones.

ARCADIA

A METAL NOVEL BY
MANDANA TOWHIDY

maybeparade

maybeparade edition

None of the bands/artists in the book or on the soundtrack have any
affiliation with the Author or the book or anything else related to the book
other than the Author loves them enough to include them and write an
entire book about the music scene.

cover & chapter titles designed by Christopher Bettig

First mass market paperback edition: 2012
10 9 8 7 6 5 4 3 2 1

m a y b e p a r a d e

PORTLAND 2012

for

PJ Mark

thank you.

and for

Bunny Olds

miss you.

Ar·ca·di·a:

any real or imaginary place offering peace and simplicity.

ARCADIA

⚡There were days I sat in 3ʳᵈ period counting dimes—I only needed 11 for a burrito from Lita. After the six block journey, cutting out of class a little early to get to Lita's and back or sometimes ditching the class entirely, I'd return to campus, hoping the narks wouldn't see me. Big Dot and Willy Valentine were always waiting to make their daily lunch busts on the backside of campus, usually non–seniors who left the grounds "without proper permissions" to smoke or toke or do whatever at Lita's.

"You're a senior, right, babe?" Big Dot would ask me as her partner Willy stood by smirking under his breath. They didn't fit into the eccentrically and ridiculously rich white snooty campus that this high school was. Big Dot wore very late '70s suits in very muted mauves and rusty colors. She was a mix of black and Hispanic or maybe purely Mexican with too much bronzer and brassy '70s hair, the color of burnt sugar that might have been a wig. But I could never tell for sure because you had to look really hard to see the plasticness in the strands and I couldn't look that hard at her for that long.

She was powerful. She and Willy always had some private party going on. And we all thought she had a good buzz going on half the time. I seemed to be on her good side because she almost always let me off the hook. Even if I was so totally busted. But I never questioned shit. Why would I?

She was a tough motherfucker. Maybe even more so than her cohort Willy. There was definitely talk flying around that he truly was a pimp. Stories were confirmed of catching Willy on the weekend in El

Monty or Dena on a backstreet bar like Boozers Hall of Fame. They always read the same way: his dark, shiny, black skin was clothed in some poly pimp–suit with a huge plumed hat atop his shiny Jheri–curl and a really pimpy tweed–ish coat with red fox collar around his shoulders and a couple of really bulbous ho–bags with missing teeth in the backseat of his car. He even joked about his big shiny pimp cane. You could easily see it. He grinned a grin that could devour you into his bloodshot eyes. There was even a rumor that he had little bottles of booze stashed all over school. I guess they got him through his day. Like I said, the stories were always the same. So we believed it.

"Yeah," I answered insecurely. I couldn't ever see Big Dot's eyes because she wore the biggest violet–tinged sunglasses. Honestly, I always felt a little bad lying to her face, especially when she'd bust the others and let me go.

Maybe Big Dot was easier on me because I hung out with a pack of senior girls or maybe it was because I was smaller than most of the other girls with my long bronze wavy 'do and puffy bangs or maybe it was because I had that innocent quality about me—that wasn't too far from the truth—with my too–big honey eyes and baby fat curves that were a result of beer and not baby at all. I did have a very good natural tan to my skin and an always–there pout. Maybe it was because, unbeknownst to me, my group of friends were the rockstars of the school. Maybe she could sense I was a little dreamer in a world filled with fake nails, fake IDs, and fake noses. And she had respect for that. Sketchwood High. Where everyone walked around with perfect bangs and perfectly horrendous blond jobs (BJ's). Sometimes I just wished I could peel back the film that covered my eyes…that plastic–y film that makes it entirely impossible to see what's real real and what's…not. The film they glue over your precious clear vision, even before you've opened your eyes. The mass–produced variety that's bottled, labeled, artificially flavored, and dyed. Whatever it was, she moved me along without any real discussion.

"You better get to class, babe, before you're late."

"OK," I replied, a little scared that I'd be totally fucked if she ever really found out I was only a junior. But, for now, I was free and it was time to jump back into the sea of drama, hair, sluts, assholes, and gossip that was the s–essence of Sketchwood High. We hated it, but it was Sketchwood and it was ours just the same. ⚡

Sketchwood had two hallways—the "main floor" and another hallway that was deemed more or less invisible or else was the equivalent of a smelly back alley way. The popular kids, jocks, misfits, rockers, skaters, surfers, and class politicians walked through the "main floor". Everyone else, including most of the Asians and people we never even knew existed, walked through the ghost–town hallway on the west side of the flat campus grounds. The only reason anyone from the main floor would ever be in that hallway would be to get to a class they had or because they wanted to avoid seeing anyone post plastic surgery or they were hiding because of major zit flare ups or from rumors brought on by drunken slutty behavior from the weekend before. People loved to dish post party—even if they weren't there. People also had affairs back there in the invisible nerdy hall. And if you were hiding in that hallway and saw someone you knew walking toward you, the both of you would avoid any eye contact and move swiftly past each other—with the unspoken agreement that neither one of you would EVER mention seeing the other to any soul for as long as you lived at Sketchwood High. There was a windy desolate stench looming through that invisible hall. If the main floor had palm trees and tropical shrubbery, umbrella–ed cocktails, bands playing flying V's, and girls dancing in French–cut boomerang bikinis atop high tables (which it didn't), then the invisible hall was definitely the alley outside the backstage door. "NO ENTRY ALLOWED, except if you're pretty, whorish, will kiss a lot of ass, or rich. In that case, enter at your own risk."

Above and beyond the two hallways, there was also the front entry onto campus, where freshmen and sophomores hung out. A place where you went to be seen. And the back entrance, for anyone *truly* cool. The backside was also reserved for Punk Rock huddles, mad dashes to Lita, smoking bushes across the street, and pickups from college boyfriends. It was, even for the popular Twinkie Twins, completely forbidden and people like them would never attempt to hang, enter, or leave from that side of the hall.

That's where my locker was. Well, my real assigned locker was right in the center of the main floor, next to the lunch and snack area. High traffic, jock assholes, and too much for me. So I adopted an abandoned space clear at the misfits' end. And, I liked it that way. No one questioned my being at that end and I was in great company, I thought. I was caught somewhere between the pretty girls and the Deadheads, skinheads, Goths, and stoners, who might not have been part of the popular cliques, but weren't invisible either. It felt good to have a foot in every door. Without even trying. I mean, I knew girls who wanted to kill each other, who despised each other, who envied each other, who cheated on each other, who smelled each other. It was heaven. I never knew where I fit in and, this way, I didn't have to decide. Being younger and smaller and quiet, people left me alone for the most part, or else they just looked out for me.

The scariest way to start the week was with the Monday morning broadcast given by the toothy whore whose goal was to get straight A's in school and straight A's in bed with all the hideous male sluts, or mutts, she got validation from, like a dented gold star right in the middle of her kooch. The rumor was that Goldie Locks, AKA one half of the Twinkie Twins, howled like a coyote in bed when her fat, no–neck pea–brain mutt boyfriend fucked her. There were a couple ways this rumor could have started:

Her blockhead boyfriend could have squealed to his clan of equally stupid, equally unattractive, equally slutty mutts so he'd look like a stud (when he obviously had no penis). The only thing he was really known for was his round face and ass and his stream of fights, also a clear sign of a dude with no pickle. He was also famous for drooling in class. He was even too dumb to play sports. And Goldie Locks already had signs of a double chin. Still, her annoying voice didn't seem to take away from her perfect body or stop the rampant fantasies boys had hoping of to hear the howl for themselves.

The other way the gossip could have started is if her fat drooling mutt was porking her drunk body in the parents' bedroom at some party *right* before she puked on the front lawn. Girls are evil. If her Goldie "friends" had heard her howl, they wouldn't have hesitated to broadcast that info out into the party so it'd be front page news at school the following Monday morning, hopefully (but unsuccessfully) making Goldie Locks look so ridiculous that other mutts would ditch her coyote/G–spot calls and come running after their bits. Stab a girl in the back so a mutt will want to pork you. I think a lot of the so–called popular girls had this motto secretly tattooed on the inside of their lips.

"WILL STAB FOR PORK."

I don't know. It's not like we hated her. She was never mean to me. In fact, she was always nice in some starfucker way because she, like most other girls, was in love with one of my good friends, a hardcore shortboard surfer who looked and acted the life as much as anyone living dead center in Hawaii or Huntington Beach. He had copped his feel on her one night, inside his late '60s yellow Bug, and then moved onto the next hot–easy–little–thing. And had he beckoned her, she would have probably dumped the drooling oaf mutt for him in a heartbeat. I guess that was all a part of the popularity game, too. Something I never could or would or had to do. I didn't really know how. I didn't ever have the hot new $200 cowboy ankle boots or wear expensive jeans or have $300 hair BJ's. My wardrobe had to be thoroughly thought out. I had a budget. A small one. I went to faraway malls and shopped in nook–and–cranny bins for a piece here and piece there. I always started with a basic set of shoes for school, which were separate from my evening party clothes. (That was a different world where almost anything goes.) One pair of white flats or loafers, and then one black, and one pair of black boots. This year my favorites were my little white penny loafers that I got on sale from Pasha's of London. They had pointy–ish narrow toes and little silver studs on the "tongue". Then my mom would take me to the fabric store where I'd choose a couple of different prints and she would make me a couple of skirts. Thank God I knew how to put an outfit together. And no one ever questioned my looks. At least not to my face. But, yeah, pretty much everyone else was at the most popular boutiques buying the most sought–after shoes and tops and all. The thing I had going for me was my mother had taste and liked how I got a little funky. I didn't really ever feel hot at school and my tops were always loose because in junior high I had blossomed from a boney grasshopper into a busty teenager. But at school I didn't want anyone to notice. Not to mention, all the Mickey's 40–ouncers packed on some 10 pounds or more by the time we reached midyear. I never really thought anything until one day at snack, Ashley said, "You always *do your own thing*. I like it." It was a surprise to hear from her. I never knew she even noticed. Our styles were so different.

"Today at snack we'll be having our first pep rally! It's Sketchwood versus Cha–Ching High at this Friday's football game! Let's go, Sketchwood Pow–Wows!" The only thing hot about school sports was the Indians.

I met Tessa in the hallway right after class and the Twinkie Twin broadcast.

"There's a party at Tommy's right now. Ash is picking us up."

"OK." Yes!

"I have to go to the bathroom first to do my lipgloss,!" she said. Tess was a prinker, a stick, and a brainiac who played the dumb blonde to a tee. When I was with her, we'd never just make a mad dash to a party without a little bit of prinking.

You have to understand, only losers went to pep rallies and only the total geeks were cheerleaders. It seemed like the freshmen girls who sucked a lot of senior jock dick were going to change that though, and I know the older lot of girls did cheerleading. But we wouldn't be caught dead at a rally and the only reason we'd show up at a game was to drink and find out where the parties were that night, anyway. Unless someone was crushing on someone or there weren't any shows happening in Hollywood. No. Pep rallies were for punters. But we loved them because it gave us enough time to head to someone's house, down a bunch of Coors Lites, smoke some bowls, eat some Lita, and MAYBE, if we had the energy, head back to class. More than often, we'd be too tired and wasted or mid–day hungover to actually get back. And I didn't drive, so my life was at the mercy of the person with the wheels. Stoned and, quite often, totally destroyed.

Tess and I went into the last bathroom at the end of the main floor. As usual, when we walked in, Taylor Twist was standing in front of the mirror, blushing her cheeks with her Wet–n–Wild $2 blush and flat square blush brush. It never mattered if she used cheap products or her hair was mushroom rockered out beyond belief. She was still always the most beautiful person ever. She had the perfect *Baywatch* body with amazing perfect boobs that sort of got thrust in your face when she hugged you. Probably because she was just a little taller than average. And maybe because she stood perfectly straight which naturally pushed them forward. She had crazy roots from her at–home BJ and her huge aquamarine eyes looked like they were plugged into 1000 volts with the Day–Glo blue contacts she wore over them. She had one million perfectly separated and curled lashes, and she always wore a little bit of *Flashdance* in her wardrobe—some tank, some cut–off pink sweatshirt on a cut–off denim micro–mini, some frosty pink lipgloss, purple glitter eyeliner (as if she needed it), white crisscross diagonally–buckled belt. No matter what, she was forever blushing or ratting her big, rocker mushroom coif. Taylor also dated the biggest Heshers in Sketchwood. And no one dare say anything bad about her. We were lucky. She adored us and we worshipped her pageant smile and Hawaiian Tropic bikini model looks.

"Hi, guys. There's a party at Tommy's."

"Yeah, we know," Tess answered adoringly. "Do you need a ride?"

"No, hon'. Tommy's picking me up. See you there." ⚡

TESS

⚡Tessa M. Schoeffling put her perfect lipgloss on. Most people didn't take her seriously. She was a flat–chested, rail thin German doll, the stretched out body of a 12 year old. Not in an anorexic way, though. She was healthy skinny, but skinny–skinny nonetheless. Tallish, maybe 5–foot–7, white as, well, Barbie. She had China doll–straight, near–Albino hair and huge dark blue eyes. She had an innocent smile with smallish teeth and was always perfectly put together. She had been the biggest Cuntempo's fan since we were too young to shop there. "The manager said when I'm 16, they'll hire me!" she had gleefully declared in 8th grade. Her textbooks were always covered in '80s Cuntempo Casuals paint–splatter book covers then, the ones they gave as gifts with purchase. I never had any of those. They matched her personality and, even as a senior, she had the same vibe as those Cuntempo's paint–splatter book covers. Same vibe. She had a not–so–tiny nose, but she was pretty enough to pull it off, even with the huge snorty laugh she belted out after a hard giggle. Tess was Duran Duran (John Taylor) and hot pink and turquoise and Tiffany bean charms and raspberry squares from Fredericko's Bakery where she worked her junior year. "Don't eat the surprise cookies," she warned quietly. "They just mix all the left over cookies into a new dough and bake it."

Today she was wearing a hot turquoise wife beater over a white wife beater over hot pink leggings belted with a white diagonal belt and turquoise pumps. She had two or three thin gold chains including a cross her psychologist mother had given to her for graduating junior high. Her bangs were feathered to the side and perfectly sealed with Aqua Net and gifted with a tiny ribbon tied just past her bangs, à la Alice in Wonderland. Even in times of grief, like when her dear friend had died in his sleep, she showed up perfectly pieced together—and still totally Tessa–ed out—in black tank atop black–and–purple leopard print leggings and thick thick eyeliner, the color of eggplant. The entire main floor's reaction was like, "Why the fuck is she wearing that…*today?*" She couldn't help it. She was who she was. And she was unapologetic about it. I wished I could be more like that. Her voice was a nasally whine, but her face and manner were always perky and positive. She never competed with the other girls in our group and she never excluded me from anything.

I remember the first time I really hung out with her in 8th grade, when I was invited to stay over after a Christmas dance. She spent nearly an hour doing my hair and makeup, an asymmetrical puffy bob, beginner–blue eyeliner and white lace fingerless gloves she loaned me to wear with my strapless white lace short slim dress with ruffles around the hips. And yes….she made me feel amazing, even though a tall skinny blonde hot pink girl could have easily been a total bitch. Totally.

After she blushed and brushed, redid her Alice–in–Wonderland bow and checked out her little teeth to make sure no gloss was on them, she squeezed a couple of cinnamon Sweet Breath drops onto her tongue and turned to me.

"Want some?"

"Okay," I said and stuck out my tongue. "Eewww–uh…" I made a bad taste face.

"I know," she said nasally and smiled with some amusement. "But Dustin might be there, and I like him." Her voice went up on "like" and back down again on "him."

That was the other thing about Tess. She either had a boyfriend or was on hot pursuit for a new boyfriend. But it was exciting to watch because she never feared rejection. Ever. Not even with her snorty laugh or nasally voice. She was our beach bunny in black glitter sunlight and though not a lot of girls outside of our group really gave her a chance, she never gave a damn. They were probably just jealous that she ate all the crap she wanted to and drank all the beer she could and was still skinnier than anyone else. They also hated her when she got super tan because the fuzz on her arms would disappear.

The first party I went to in 7th grade, I remember seeing Tess walk out and take a flat hard dive forward onto the lawn. She was *that* drunk. She didn't cry about it later or get embarrassed. She only gave up that snorty laugh as if she was gasping for the little bit of oxygen left in that tiny body.

Tess had a collection of candy–colored Guess jeans, size 2 and 3, and jelly shoes to match. She did her homework in her teal wife beater, gold charms, ribbon, and hot pink Cuntempo's string bikini panties, her blonde pubes peeking out of the sides.

Then Tess took out her blush brush and put a little dusty rose bronzer on the apples of my cheeks.

"I like how this looks on you, Ronnie. But you're already naturally tan. You don't really need very much," and smiled sweetly. I just smiled back. It was nice to not have to do anything. That's probably why I always took refuge at her mom's condo every time I ran away from home. Because everything felt effortless there.

"I don't think The Fang will be there, though. I don't really need to look perfect," I mumbled in a low heartsinking way, sort of admitting my crush on the 21–year–old roadie (and son of the most successful lawyer in Dena.)

"That's okay. You'll see him at the show this weekend. And there are other boys, too, you know."

"I know." But I didn't know. But somehow, she did. She had this other sense about her that saw you in the future, and it was always a happy portrait. Fulfilled and fucked hard.

"I know you might not think it, but he likes you. He does. I think you should just have some fun with all the other guys who like you."

"Yeah…" I mumbled like air seeping out of a hole in a tire. "I don't know…it's hard." Tess stopped her blushing and turned toward me again.

"Ron, come on. You've never seen me crying over a guy like an asshole? We all go through it." And then she opened her stormy ocean eyes at me, almost looking up even though she was looking down, and smiled her little teeth smile. The same smile in cheerleading pictures of her from 2nd grade, looking up with her pom–poms on her hips. Same little teeth.

She said nothing for those few seconds. I just looked back at her. I wanted to believe her. But I didn't know how much of it was true. Then she put a little more blush on me and threw her stuff in her white fringe bag and zipped it.

"You know…a lot of guys like you," she said. "Come on. Ash'll leave without us if we make her wait and I wanna get to that party. I wanna see if she'll stop by Bananas Over Yogurt before we get beer. And I want to get cigarettes."

I sighed in the cold mirror and fluffed my puffy bangs, looking myself right in the eyes. "Okay. I'm ready." And we were out the door. ⚡

⚡ Ash was waiting in her supersonic, detailed, and raised Big Red Bronco, music blaring. Ezze was sitting shotgun like always and smiling at us with an eyebrow up as we rushed in quick skips, Tess pulling at my wrist. Ash looked eerily pissed and constipated, she was impatient as always. Even if we were a minute late, she looked ready to tell you off. I guess it was the power of her Big Red Penis, or her tree–length limbs, that fed her ego. But as soon as we climbed in, she cracked a deep dimpled smile and in a softer raspy voice said, "Let's get some beer and fuck–ing party!" She was always pro at DJing in her car with the homemade mixed tapes that we listened to nonstop.

"We don't have to get beer," Tess mumbled passively. "There's a keg at Tommy's."

"Okay," Ash mouthed back in her I–have–money–but–I–have–to–sound–trailer–trash voice. "But there better be beer when we get there 'cause I'm not leaving to score beer." Tess didn't want to deal with Ash's power bullshit, and she didn't understand why anyone else had to, either. It was the reason why, even though Tess liked Ash, she usually chose to drive herself or go with her flavor–of–the–moment. But this was snack, way early in the day, and we might've gone back to school afterwards, depending on how wasted we got or how good the party was, of course.

"Well, if you want to get something to be safe since we're right by Star Liquor…"

"Naaaah. Let's just go. We should've already been there by now," Ash mumbled back. She really didn't mean to be such a bitch. But despite her twinkly blue eyes, freckles and sandy blonde looks, she couldn't let go of the motorhead butch inside of her. And, she did always drive. So we didn't care. Just before the Big Red Bronco pulled away, we saw Sydney running over.

"Your little ass is lucky, bitch," Ash smirked with a tinge of sarcasm. "We almost left you behind."

But Sydney didn't give a fuck. She just ignored Ash because she knew Ash wouldn't dare leave her behind. Ash loved Ezze, and Ezze's number one was always Sydney. So Syd played it off and offered her staple silly relief.

"Fuck, my koochie's itching! I need to get waxed!" Sydney laughed.

"Where's the rake?"

Syd giggled. "I just need a fucking drink!"

The party had already started and we hadn't even pulled away from the curb. Ezze sat shotgun and Sydney sat in back next to Tess and me. The two tiny ones and the tiny tall one. And everyone in the car was blonde except me. Syd was laughing her bracey smile.

"Let's fucking party!" Syd shouted with her mousy yelp.

⚡When we got to Tommy's house, it looked like a hundred cars had beat us there. Every inch of the long crescent manicured driveway was now landscaped with raised white and black Jeep Wranglers with furry zebra seat covers, gold and champagne Mercedes, red Beamers, white Beamers, black Porsches, raised red 4x4s pickups that looked like disco balls, T–Top bitchin' Camaros, IROCS, black convertible Cabriolets, white Sciroccos, little red Corvettes, T–Top Firebirds, and even an Alpha Romero or two. This was the land of parentless houses, bottomless kegs, and beer bong mountains. No matter how huge or scandalous the parties got or how many times the cops showed up, it never mattered. There was always a very vacant house waiting for

300 soon–to–be drunk kids to show up at, and they were always huge many–many–roomed mansions with multi–car garages, crystal–blue tiered pools, half–acre lawns with the strange lawn jockeys greeting the pissers and pukers who made their jockeyed acquaintances. And quite often they, literally, had intense conversations or crying sessions with the clowny statuettes. Even though there was always music blasting, I could never make it out very well. It always felt drug–induced and coked out. Though I had personally never seen the stuff, I knew it was always around.

Ash made her own parking space—right in the middle of the flower beds crawling with heirloom roses in pink and peach and lined with imported bricks.

"Oh well. No one's going to fuck with my car." She was right. No one would dare come near her car. She was a dragonlady to some, with her ever–long legs, ever–long acrylic nails, and ever–sharp tongue.

We pulled out our lipgloss, then blush brushes, powder brushes (we powdered all the time, and it had to be loose powder…usually Clinique) and then ratted our bangs and the tops of our crown and back of our heads. Ash pulled out spray and spritzed her bangs so they'd stay awake. Ezze sprayed each side so it stayed to the side and out a bit, and Sydney sprayed anywhere haphazardly she could dig her hot pink nails into—she was *that* cute and *that* confident. She was going out with Ezze's much older brother, so she didn't really have to give a fuck. Tessa didn't do a thing except touch up the gloss on the bottom of her frosty pink lips. Then she looked at me and whispered, "You look cute. Let's go. Open the door." I wasn't sure if my big long brown curly mane was right on or not, but I trusted her. She had never let me down since I had met her in the 7th grade. I looked up into the rearview mirror to gage where Ash's attention was. She was still fucking with her thin long perky bangs. Sometimes she was more insecure than the other girls whenever we arrived at a party. I opened the door, got out and adjusted my black–n–white checkerboard stretch denim miniskirt as I peered down to my scrunched white socks and black–n–white Creepers. Tess slid out of the Big Red Bronco with her thinness and hot pink and turquoise number. She had a hot pink bow in her hair. Tess always matched.

She motioned for me to follow her. The other girls were barely getting out of the car. They were probably annoyed we were walking away—except for Sydney who never cared and was closest to Ezze anyway. Like, I don't know if Tess would have ever really become friends with Ash if Ezze hadn't first. Ezze and Syd went way back because their families were friends and Syd's mom was Ezze's drama teacher when she was little. And Tess and I had been friends since we were like 11 or so. And Tess and Syd were cheerleaders in junior high. So Ezze and Syd became friends and I quickly clicked in. Ash was the latecomer. None of us even knew of her until we started high school.

As we approached the door to one of the Tommy's houses, we could hear some commotion and smell what was familiar to us—the distinct waft of spilt Budweiser mixed in with the smell of pot and cigarettes. It was never a party until we arrived though. We did always go to the best parties and the most secret get–togethers, no poseurs or dumb girls allowed. No jocks, no idiots. Occasionally some would show up and try to bond with us. But then they'd end up replacing that very big stick up their very tight assholes the moment we got back to school. No. This was our territory and we were young, hot, and... free. At least for the morning. ⚡

Entering the million dollar party estate—i.e. Tommy's—was like entering into a dark smoky tunnel, even though it wasn't even noon yet and sunny as any Southern Cali suburb day. It never seemed to matter which Tommy was having a party or how well we knew any of them. If there was a party at Tommy's, we'd be there—everyone would be there—and we knew the party'd be good, which meant a lot of people would get laid and *everyone* would be fucked up. It didn't matter if we should have been watching some cheerleaders dance some dumb routine to the same Yaz song they always did their dumbass routines to: pom–poms left to right...right to left...left up right down...blah blah. We acted like we were at a bar, filling up our plastic cups with frothy Bud. Only in Sketchwood could the Tommy's produce a full keg at a moment's notice in the middle of the morning. Only 15 minutes ago we were being subjected to some dank, double–chin broadcast about geeky high school life inside concrete classrooms.

Here, it was about the smell of weed and pork in the bathroom. Or, other things in the bathroom. Whenever we went to a party, almost instantly one of the girls would say, "Ronnie, so–and–so is going to smoke you out in the back." Okay, I always replied gleefully. I was younger and babied and maybe naïve. These girls took care of me and made sure I went straight to the back where there'd be a circle of misfit stoners or some much older partiers or just a couple of kids I knew from Modern Poetry class. I left the girls, went to the back porch, and saw Dave and Melissa smiling at me along with one of the Tommy's and some other people I didn't know. "Wanna get high?" Yeah.

I took three long chatty hits and was laughing uncontrollably. Then, I glided back toward the rec' room, passing the bathroom, or one of the bathrooms, when the door opened and Tess, Ezze, and Ash walked out with Taylor and Devon behind them.

"What are you guys doing?" my wide eyes said. I felt a little confused and left out. But, I figured they had just gone in to do their hair…maybe.

"Nothing, babe," Ezze offered as she caressed and styled the hair that had fallen on the sides of my face. "Nothing. Did Dave get you high?"

"Yeah! I'm hiiiigh!" I laughed. "I have to pee."

"Okay, little one. Come find me when you're done." She puckered her lips and I gave her a little affectionate peck. Ash's eyes were bugged out and she stared at me with a bit of a psychotic smile.

I went into the bathroom and closed the door and Tess came back inside with me. ⚡As I peed all the beer out, I watched Tess pull out her makeup bag. She put mascara on mascara and lipgloss over lipgloss and blush over blush and electric–blue liner on the insides of her electric-blue lined eyes and opened her mouth a bit, pressing her teeth together, and with her huge blue blinkless eyes staring into the mirror, rubbed the front of her teeth with her pointer finger, as if to wipe away the gloss. But no gloss was on her teeth. Then, still hunched over the sink, her nose almost touching the mirror that covered the entire wall lodged between the cornflower blue walls, she pressed her tongue over the front of her teeth and under her top lip. All the while, I peed and watched.

"Do I need more gloss?" I asked as I wiped and pulled up my mini. She paused—I think—for a minute and with—I think a delayed response—answered, "Here." She turned to me as I was still pulling up my skirt and rubbed the frosty pink gloss sponge applicator wand over my lips. Her eyes were wide. Really wide. And she was still rubbing her tongue on the front of her teeth.

"There's–that–party–in–Dena–on–Saturday–Are–you–going–I'm–not–sure–I'm–going–to–that–but–we're–all–going–to–the–Repulsors'–party–on–Friday–and–there's–the–show–at–The–Troubadour–too–I–think–the–girls–are–going–but–I'm–not–going–to–that–either–I'm–going–to–the–beach–Do–you–have–a–fake–ID–yet–You–have–your–fake–ID–right–You–look–cute–Come–on–We–should–see–if–they're–ready–to–go–back–I'm–getting–hungry–Do–you–want–Lita?"

I just shrugged my shoulders. Tess was still pressing her tongue over the front of her teeth lip as though they were giving off some great flavor. I realized she had no clue what she was doing. Or else, I was confused as to why she was doing it for so long and still able to talk so fast and ask me so many questions, simultaneously. Her gold loop earrings were vibrating a little bit, too.

"Yeah, I've had a fake ID for six months now. It says Kodak on the back, but no one has said anything." My friend's cousin Peter had gotten it for me from someone at work. It cost me thirty bucks. I met Peter at CoCo's coffee shop after school one day to pick it up. My name on the ID read:

CONCHITA LERNER. CONCHITA LERNER? And I was 27 years old. The picture I had supplied them with was tiny and looked much darker. And then there was the Kodak logo paper all over the back. But, I was at the point of no return and out thirty bucks. It was better than nothing. I wasn't lucky enough to have an older sister I could "inherit" or steal an ID from. They were the lucky ones, because whenever any bouncer tested them, they knew all the answers. For the rest of us, we had to memorize the fake address and the zodiac sign and the fake birthdate. They didn't use any of your info, they'd just slap your picture onto someone else's probably–stolen driver's license. So we had to memorize everything, which sucked when you were drunk or high and getting questioned because of course we got nervous and looked totally unnatural. And not 27. But, I had been nearly everywhere with it…every gay dance club, every surf bar, everywhere. Thank God my quiet side and big boobs took care of me. Or else we were always with some group of guys who were over 21. Not random dudes—but the same guys we usually partied with on the weekends. The same guys who scored our booze for us when we were in junior high.

"Why aren't you going to the show? You never go," I asked, feeling very hungry and tired and a bit something.

"I'm going to the beach. Come on," she motioned to me with a waving hand to follow her again.

We walked back into the sea of hair, smoke, and French country duck maroon green plaid—this was the land of Dooney&Burke (or Dooky&Pork as I liked to call it) after all. It always fascinated me the way we could just take over a clearly tidy home and have literally everything and anything happen in a matter of two or three hours, then leave the aftermath for someone else to clean up. The homes always got trashed. I mean, how did they do it? Everyone's parents were away at some point, and they always left the kids to fend for themselves with a couple of stocked freezers in their three–car garages and plenty of rooms where everyone was getting porked, snorting coke or even crystal, vomiting in the kitchen sink, spilling beer at every syllable (which was always a sign that the party started right) and pissing in the bushes, on the lawn, and even in the pools. No matter how well I cleaned up, my parents would have known 100 kids were in their house. But, luckily for me, I never had to throw a party or worry about the post–party destruction because everyone else's parents were too caught up in their own parental worlds away at their cabins, on their cruises, or Waikiki getaways.

When we walked out of the cornflower blue bathroom, Taylor was going in, again, comb in hand, to rat her hair.

"Hey, guys. Are you going back? I'm so fucked up." If Taylor hadn't ended up a rocker, she would have definitely had pom–poms in her locker. She just had that perky "Hey–Guys–What's–Up" thing about her. All the time.

"Yeah, I think so," Tess answered.

"Well, I think Ash is ready to go if you need a ride."

Tess and I walked down the hallway, past family portraits of Tommy and his family framed in more duck plaid. Toothy smiles. Dumbassness. I followed Tess. I was still stoned and, for some reason, a little warm. My eyes were burning from cigarette smoke and even though the music was loud and hard to make out, I still banged my head a little. In an hour, we had destroyed the house. But this Tommy was still smiling his toothy Tommy smile just like the portraits and talking to Ezze and Ash when we walked toward them through the fog and stench. Ash had that impatient quirk in her tiny chiseled nose again. But I don't think it had anything to do with getting back to class. Ezze was smiling her flower child love smile and, as usual, listening but didn't really care what Tommy was rambling on about. She was licking the front of her teeth and touching the front of her teeth, but in a little more relaxed way than Tess.

"Where's Sydney?" Tess asked. Ezze smiled her orgasmic lazy smile, started playing with the sides of Tessa's hair, running her wine–colored acrylics through the stick–straight hair behind Tessa's ears, still licking the front of her teeth occasionally.

"She left with Jake. She's not going back to school and I don't know if we are either. Do you need a ride back?"

"Yeah. I need to take a test." Then Tess looked at me. I had been standing there next to them quietly, as usual. Watching, listening, looking, waiting. "Are you coming back with me? Come back with me," she insisted sweetly.

"Yeah, I have to go back." I said.

But the truth is, after getting straight A's effortlessly my entire life, skipping two grades, and bypassing beginner courses, I had started to not care about school. I really didn't give a fuck anymore. School had been so easy for me. And so, it seemed just as easy not go to class or not care. And fake a note to get back in. I never discussed it with anyone. I was the only one in my clique in high math and honors English and even advanced art classes. But I hated math. It was so uncreative and boring as hell. And the teachers were all HUGE assholes. Especially in high school. At least in junior high we got the comedy of watching Mrs. Wiggums move her cheap curly fro wig back to scratch her head. And with her thick bottle glasses, it was just too cartoon to not love it. Anyway, I just didn't really care and I guess part of me was hoping someone would ask what was wrong. What had happened. But really no one ever did. The only person who said anything was my old buffoon ultra–white pointy–nosed neckless bald counselor. "Look," he had said, pointing to the long history of all my A's and B's and then pointing to the 1st quarter progress report grades, which were all D's and C's and even an F. "Are you having problems at home?" There it was. Finally. "Yeah," I mumbled back—looking at him dead center in the eyes as if to beg him to really probe me for more. But all I got was a deadpan face that froze on me with almost prejudice pity. "Oh," he said. And that was it. Nothing. A lot of times I thought there'd be more concern from the school faculty had I been blond with a couple of nose jobs and had a last name that was prefixed with Van or something like that. Most teachers and staff just chalked it up to my being foreign and living in an apartment or else they didn't even know. They only speculated. There were only a couple of teachers who really got me, and I adored them. But so did everyone else.

"I think I'm just going to Mrs. T's. I'll just get the test review study notes from Mr. LeGrady tomorrow," I answered in a very stony way. "Can we get frozen yogurt first?" ⚡

ASH

⚡ Ashley K. Manning was a walking paradox. She was the zebra–striped giraffe of our bunch. And she had the teeth to grind.

The first memory I have of actually "connecting" with Ash was walking next to her in the hallway toward the student parking lot. Before that, I hardly ever paid attention to her—in a very positive way, that is. I knew who she was. But before I really knew her, I just stayed away because Ash was a loud tree, and her name was always associated with kicking someone's ass. It wasn't until she broke her gentle twinkly smile that I'd see her softer underbelly. She seemed so hard–to–touch and kind of lower class, even though she loved and could afford lots of strapless North Beach Leather dresses. Maybe because the rest of us went to the same Hoity Toity junior high school in the foothills. I don't know how she befriended the rest of the girls, but they must have bonded over something in class like how much they hated the modern dance teacher who up and abandoned us one day after she landed a part in a Madonna video or maybe it was how much they hated the idiot volleyball girls who lived on a diet of Crystal Lite and tanning salon sessions that hit "visit #144" before the middle of the year was even near or maybe they just loved each other's nails and hair and love of sex and Metal.

Anyway, the first real connection I made with her started off really weird. We were both walking the same way and I think she came up from behind me—because she was walking really fast and she was 6 feet tall and most of that was her legs. She had the prettiest heart shaped petite mouth and perfect cleft chin and white–light clear blue eyes. She was wearing a peach tie–dyed cropped T–shirt and a white knit mini skirt and lots of jewelry on her long fingers, bangles on her wrists, and big hoop earrings, and had the sides of her hair pulled up into an equally sparkly barrette atop her head just behind her bangs which were sprayed to stay up a bit. She was barefooted with her shoes in her bag, which we all did sometimes because we were only a 20–minute drive from the beach. She was walking at a really rapid pace, with her staple huge ESPRIT white canvas bag, filled with her school books and hairspray cans, no doubt, thrown over one shoulder and her drawstring white leather purse swathed with fringe and silver studs over the other shoulder. Her long almost–chola nails were airbrushed the same peachy tangerine orange as her top, and she was pounding one fist into the other palm, then stretching her fingers and cracking her knuckles at the same rapid pace as her walk.

"I'm going to kick some motherfuckin' ass! Fuck yeah! No one takes my man! No one!" At first I thought she was serious as I slowly looked back a bit over my shoulder. Like I said, I only knew she was always talking about kicking someone's ass. She caught up and was now walking right next to me. My thought was...she was crazy!

"Bo's my man and I'm kicking some ass!" Then she cracked a little smile at me. Which finally made some sense. Bo wasn't her man, but he was beautiful and graduated and a model for reals and probably had nothing to do with her. So it was clear she was just being silly. I smiled back. And that was that.

She loved dance music, but really couldn't dance for shit. She was just too damn tall. But she did really want to be a model, and she could have been if she hadn't tried so hard. Her photos were contrived finger–in–the–corner–of–her–slightly–opened–mouth, hand–on–hip poses. Maybe it would have helped if she didn't hunch over the way she did which kept her from looking graceful and always made me think of the word lanky. But she was cute enough and tall enough. She was the daughter of a motorhead tyrant and she had been racing four–wheelers since the age of 2. Ash was too tall for jeans and her feet were size 11's. She could be really mean and demanding, but as soon as she broke a smile, everything turned California sunshine. Aside from anything, she loved teal and white and she watched out for her girls. And we loved that. She also loved sex and talking in detail about sex and having sex. Once after a Halloween party, she and Ezze and I traveled 40 minutes to the East Hills to hang out with the little brother of a rockstar from the biggest Metal band (from our neck of the woods) and party in his big brother's rockstar mansion. After we toured the place, Ash fucked one of his friends right there in the rec room on the pool table next to a stack of gold and platinum records that hadn't even been taken out of their shipping boxes yet. Aside from that, she was obsessed with a friend of The Fang who sometimes treated her like an angel, but most of the time treated her like hell. At least that's how he acted in front of us. He was a smart driven rocker musician with long bushy hair and a very funny sense of humor, but he wasn't even really good looking or as tall as she was, which made everything worse. And I never understood any of it.

Most of the time when we ditched class, we ended up at Ash's house, because her parents were usually away at the races in a desert somewhere. Sydney and I immediately peeled a huge banana each and opened the super-sized too-fucking-huge peanut butter jar we found in the pantry. This was a ritual at Ash's. We'd top each banana bite with a spoon of chunky peanut butter, nearly finishing the jar by the time we were done talking. Today, they were talking about sex *again*. And, as always, Ash was pricking my brain. No, not picking. *Pricking*. She couldn't get over her fascination with my being a virgin. We started watching *9 1/2 Weeks* and somewhere between the peanut butter bananas and the hooker scene, she looked over at me and probed, "Don't you ever just get horrrrrr–ny?" Her eyes bugging out at the "horrrrr."

I didn't know what to say. I didn't talk about how I had been getting myself off since I was 12 or that, yeah, you don't have to actually bone to feel "horrrrrr–ny." I hated that word, anyway. I just looked at her with no expression and shrugged my shoulders, which made her go off for 10 minutes about how she couldn't believe I was a virgin especially since I always went out with older guys. I felt stupid sitting there. Eventually, Ezze and Syd gave Ash a look to lay off. They actually liked that I was pure. They did everything they could to keep it that way. Whenever we were away on spring break, like at Balboa

Island, and some guy wanted to whoosh me away to the bonfires, Ezze or Syd would say "Nuh–uh" or else they'd hook up with one of the dude's friends just so they'd be close enough to make sure the boys never tried anything crazy with me. Maybe Ash didn't realize that. She was from a sexually advanced planet in my book. THE PLANET of HORRRR–NEEE…where you fucked your boyfriend as much as you could and when you were on the rag and your period was too heavy, you douched in the shower and screwed him that way. Then you douched again and screwed again. Shower. Douche. Fuck. Douche Fuck Shower. Douche Style.

And later on at some surprise birthday party, she dared me to remove the Coors Lite label from the slightly wet bottle without tearing it. "If you tear it, then you lose your virginity tonight!" It peeled off easily and perfectly and she smiled but was pissed. I wore the Coors Lite silver label stuck to my forehead the rest of the night as a sign of my chastity. Even when Ezze walked up to me at 2 a.m. and said, "Happy Birthday. The Fang is here," the label still remained stuck to my forehead until he left three hours later.

Sitting around with Ash was always a little awkward at first. I don't know why I always expected that initial "um" moment to not be there whenever we ended up in a space alone together. Of course I expected it to not be there. But, a lot of the times, it would just rear it's ugly face in between us, and we'd have to struggle to get back to feeling "normal" again. *Especially* when I ended up shotgun.

"Don't you have any Ratt?" I'd ask. I had to start somewhere. It helped when I threw her the ball.

"Yeah. I have some Ratt somewhere in there," she said pointing to the glove box. I shuffled through a few mixed tapes until she grabbed one out of my hand and shoved it into the slit. Then Ash grinned. "This is good." ⚡

"Yeah." I looked out the window of her Big Red Bronco.

"So," she started to softly say, "You and Smiley never boned?"

"What?"

"You and Smiley..."

"Almost, a couple of times..."

"Was he too big for you? I *heard*..." she said and laughed with a jab to my shoulder. I sat there looking back at her. "But why? I thought you went out with him a couple of times..."

"I might have. I really liked him. He was so cute to me at first but then he turned into a jerk both times."

"Is it true? The reason why they call him Smiley?"

"What reason?"

"You know...that the hole in his peewee looks like a smile?"

"What? I don't know..." But I did know, or I thought I might know.

"Whatever, fuck–im! Smiley's a selfish fuck! Fuck–im! Fuck–em all!" she bellowed out and, with a full arm swing, turned the ignition. "I think it's rad that you don't bone..." Then she looked over at me with her hands on the wheel and her foot on the gas. "But, fuck, *I'd* never wanna be a virgin again!" ⚡

Ash dropped Tess and me off at Bananas Over Yogurt and took off with Ezze and Syd. After getting my half–coffee, half–cheesecake covered with Heath bits and mini butterscotch and white chocolate chips, we started walking the three long blocks back toward school. It was feeling really warm now and our school bags felt heavy and constricting. I was too tired to think and I had so much cotton–mouth, the yogurt tasted heavenly but made my mouth even drier, making me even more thirsty and uncomfortable.

"She could have taken us to school. It's on her way. That's why I don't usually like to ride with her," Tess was saying, but she wasn't pouting. She was more like me. We really didn't like games and we didn't understand nonsense power trips.

"Yeah. But Ash always wants to drive," I said, fidgeting in the bottom of my bag, hoping to find 50 cents for a bottle of Diet Orange Crush.

"I know. But then she gets over it and we're stuck walking three blocks in the heat."

Yeah. Heat. Not too bad. But after an hour of drinking and smoking and whatever else, who had the energy? Most of the kids wouldn't go back to school unless they had to. Most of us had our system locked down, knowing when and how to get back into class, blowing off the rules without ever getting caught.

I was tired. Tess wasn't, but she was agitated. She kept rubbing her elbow and she threw more than half of her baby–sized frozen yogurt into a roadside trash can. She rarely ate and had all the skinny tricks in hand like pouring water on your unfinished plate. Really crazy shit I had never heard of before meeting them. Before meeting her.

Then she took out her pink frosty lipgloss wand and applied her already–there already–glossed lips with more gloss. It must have tasted good or else it might have been a nervous habit. But that would mean there was someone at school who was making her nervous. But Tess had a boyfriend who was older—so I think this glossing meant something. This wasn't just tongue pressing. This was making pretty and trying to be coy about it and thinking I was too fucked up to notice. But I did. At this point, I was tired and sloppy. It seemed so not worth the effort of leaving for a party that ended before lunch. We got back to the main floor back door just when people were shuffling off to class. Perfect timing, except Tess's boyfriend pulled up in his beige 4x4. Tess smiled, waved, and jumped in the front seat before anyone could blink. I just stood there, scowling a clear "I'm the only fucking one who's going back to class???" look back at her. Fuck. Whatever. Fuck it.

I decided to fuck class and instead take refuge in my safe place, Mrs. T's art room. I could stay there and work and paint and talk and she didn't care. In fact, she loved me. I had gone and die–cut dancing bears in shop class and then I'd ditch a class and go into Mrs. T's art room and paint them swirly green and psychedelic pink and orange, marker their faces in black and give them away.

Entering Mrs. T's classroom was like walking into a big, warm fuzzy womb. Where no one would tug at you and no one would bother you and all your silly little Tempera and pottery clay dreams could come true. Even if you had cramps that doubled you over or a subtle black eye or bruises on your elbow and wrist that ached and should have probably been in a sling. Even if none of the other teachers noticed, you still knew. But when you were in Mrs. T's class, you forgot and felt safe and good. You believed.

Mrs. Hunny T. was amazing. She was dorky and sweet and totally rad at the same time, and *everyone* loved her. She wasn't Hoity

Toity like the other art instructor. I had taken Mrs. Goldframes (AKA Miss Nelson) class—actually been placed in her "high art" class and bypassed the beginner art classes when I was a freshman because an art teacher in junior high said I should. But, fuck. After Mrs. Hoity Toity Goldframes' class, I never pursued art again…in a serious way. It was career and college preparation and portfolios and many critiques and egos and teacher's pets and seniors. Too many seniors. I hated it. But Mrs. T's was an art class and moreover—a crafty class—for everyone. The fancy and the simple and the talented and weak kids. Even the bitchy girls and the jocks and the in–the–closet heartthrobs and especially the LSD nerdy misunderstood punks with huge curly hair that fell over their faces and onto their plaid flannel shirts. Even them and even the skaters.

Mrs. T was lovable and she got along well with the misfits. She looked like she stepped out of a 1968 Mod scooter gang. She was very tree–like to me or else she looked tree–esque. She had very jet–black bouffant–esque long hair, like Priscilla, that waved and curled in stiffish layers all the way down to her armpits, perfectly framing her awkward face. It looked like she should be standing in a mini and Go–Go boots, but she wore her flared–leg, floral '60s two–piece suits, and crafting aprons over those. She had rad chunky long hippy necklaces with huge ceramic or wood beads and big surreal rings with boulders for stones because, of course, Mrs. T was also a jewelry maker. Her skin was powdered to look ghostly white and her large almost–black brown eyes had lots of lashes with lots of black mascara. Her lips were pale or bare like the tone of her face, also very mod. And her voice was very wavy and a little hoarse and we loved that, too. It was like she knew exactly where we were all heading, and so, she just had a little more patience for the sometimes–frustrating roles and games in our lives right now. She could see where the true beauty was and, a lot of the time, it was with the ones all the other teachers prejudiced. Where some kids got shafted and scowled at by the other grownups—no matter what was really in their hearts—I think Mrs. T looked at the very same kids with gentle x–ray vision— the kind that blows gentle dandelion seed wishes along in the sun. She couldn't help but actually care for these neglected pups.

I didn't usually pay attention to the other kids when I was taking sanctuary in her class. There were always people I shared stories and laughed with, but outside of those classroom walls, they were pretty much strangers to me. Or else, that's how I played it. Or sometimes I'd see them in the main floor and want to say hi, but they'd not look my way. I guess they thought I'd just ignore them anyway. But there were a couple that I ended up good friends with. There was Paul, the Charlie Sexton–ish Death Rocker with lighter–than–light eyes. Countless freshmen girls outwardly obsessed over his quiet and genuine demeanor. He was a loner. But it didn't seem to affect him. Then there was Matty who, after only a month, broke down in whispers that his very cute but very young girlfriend was pregnant. I got her an appointment at Planned Parenthood, held her hand, and his, too. After that incident, we knew we'd be friends for life. He was a diehard Deadhead who made green gel and used to be a very preppy surf brat with his HUGE Mick Jagger eyes. Matty reminded me of a childhood friend named Michael who wore thick glasses and had tadpoles in a jar on a table in his living room and made mud dinosaurs with me on his porch in the hot sun. ϟ

We thought most of the other kids reeked of fakeness or were just a waste of time, but then there were a couple of people who were invisible to everyone. Like this girl who sat near Mrs. T's desk. Sometimes I looked at her from the corners of my eyes. I don't know who started it, but 8th grade rumors claimed she had lost her virginity on the Disneyland trip, after we went on Pirates of the Caribbean, to a boy who had popped the cherry of almost every tweeny girl. He looked all the part of a suave good–looking Mafioso, even at that age. But after that, everyone just called her Caribbean Queen, which was just her sucky ass luck 'cause that terrible song played all the time and merely destroyed her life.

Other than those two—Matty and Paul—I never really cared about anyone else in the class.

Mrs. T's class felt like camp with paint and clay and cut paper and '60s art all over the room like it was her house. And it was a large, large room—much larger than Hoity Toity Goldframes's up the hall. Everything was family style and out for everyone to work with. There was always a project and lessons, but after you were done, you could work on whatever you wanted to. Or else, you could hover over Mrs. T's desk and wait until it was your turn to tell her your life story and even get boy advice. It always felt normal and okay to have these thoughts and feelings after you spoke with her about them. I even told her when I left a note in Surfer Boy's locker that said I'd always had a crush on him and that he always made me nervous, which was probably the biggest thing I ever did. But Mrs. T thought it was sweet and cute and fun and wanted me to update her nearly every time I saw her, which was almost every day. I could tell her my dreams and talk about hair and tell her who I loved and problems in classes and everything. And she always remained quiet when you were talking and looked right at you wide–eyed—and then made a big sigh when you were finished if the news was heavy or sad or you were struggling. Sometimes she'd answer all the art questions from the hoverers, and I'd just wait quietly on the stool next to her like I was her teacher's aide. Of course she must have known I was stoned and had been drinking. My perfect outfit and lipgloss couldn't really hide what she could see.

After the last Deadhead and skinhead Mormon (both of whom I loved) had gone back to their tables, she looked at me and pushed a smile as though she'd next say, "I'll roll us a dooby." But she just said, "What's going on, Ronnie?" in the most caring voice I had ever heard.

"I don't know. I don't feel very well." She was a good mother and always sympathized with me, no matter if I was faking. But I wasn't faking this time. I knew why I didn't feel so good.

"Well, any new news? Did you see that boy?"

"Which boy?" I wanted to make sure she remembered even though she always remembered. She sat on her swivel chair and placed her hands over each other on her desk, then going through grade books, then hands going through her hair. She also usually chewed gum and clicked it slickly to the point where you thought she had batteries in the back of her neck.

"The boy that you said you wanted to take to the dance. The cute one with the dimples. He's older, I think," she whispered out of the corner of her mouth as she leaned toward me on her left.

"Oh, *that* boy. I guess I'll see him this weekend or tonight maybe. But for sure at this party. He called to tell me about it. That means 'meet me there'," I told Mrs. T. I was barely 17 and he was 21. "The Fang."

She smiled. "The Fang? What's that? You don't really call him 'The Fang', do you?" Then she stood up to make a little announcement. The students had noticed her preoccupied and there was a rambunctious vibe in the womb that Mrs. T had to quell. "Brion, Alfonso, Effie," she called attention to three young Punkers giggling playfully in the corner. Two of them had death bangs and the other was more Rockabilly with an "Elvis Hitler" pomp. They stopped and listened immediately. "If you're all done making your ceramic pencil holder or planter, you can start glazing them as soon as they're dry. If you don't have anything to do, and you cleaned your station, you can start sketching a design for the ring project." Her voice sounded like she had three frogs in her throat. One for every note.

"Yeah. He's The Fang. It just rhymes with his last name. Ashley Manning and Ezze always say that he put his fangs into me and that was it. He and I are sort of there but then I never know. He's very quiet. But, yeah, ironically, his name rhymes with The Fang." She just smiled. It was nice to just tell a story to Mrs. T and have her smile back at me and I didn't have to lie or feel like I did something wrong or stupid, and that my little crush was interesting and important to her.

"Well, I want to see a picture. So when the dance comes, I want you to save me a picture." She sounded like only two frogs were in her throat now. Maybe one escaped.

THE PANG

The Fang was a beautiful creature who would break my heart forever, just like every high school mystery lover. ⚡

It was phone calls and silly little laughs and bong hits and Steel Pulse and Van Halen and on and off and on and off and on and on and on and off and on and off again. It was subtle Goliath gestures and confusing intermissions and keeping me at arms length—just close enough to sense a pulse and feel his breath at the nape of my neck, but with enough space reserved between us for a thousand "IN CASE OF EMERGENCY, PLEASE BREAK THIS UP" excuses. ⚡

I had met The Fang totally by accident at one of the parties Ash, Ezze, Taylor, Devon, Sydney, and I had gone to following a Repulsors' party. We had gone straight to the cottage mansion with a garden–wedding backyard. It was beautiful with white bricks and rose boxes, oak trees, and plenty of French iron benches so you could sit in the warm moonlight. The older boys were at the party and so were all the skaters, who were older, too. Somehow, in my drunken wobbles, I had declared that I liked Buck Henry to everyone. Buck Henry was a lot older, like 25, and danced in dips a lot like Jim Morrison. He looked like him, too, but with shorter hair. I remember some annoying surf jock with braces that lots of girls crushed on (though I never thought he was hot) kept giving me shit about Buck and my tights. "They're navy, but you're pretending they're black," he kept saying. I didn't know if he was flirting or being a dick, but I didn't care because my drunken sights were set on Buck. I had no idea something else was waiting for me on the other side of that party. I first "met" The Fang and hour or so later when I ran to that part of the yard that was still under landscape construction. The girls and some of the boys that I didn't know yet stood right on top of dirt mounds that looked a lot like coffee grounds.

I tried to balance my wobbly self atop the cocoa humps facing the boys, but I kept sliding around in my black steel–toe stilettos, "fake black navy tights," and little black Lycra dress. The Mickey's 40–ouncer made it harder to balance because the bottle was so damn heavy, and it slipped out of my hand onto the ground in front of the boys. In an attempt to catch it, I, too, nearly landed at their feet.

"Whooooa!" and laughter is all I heard. I hadn't even had a moment to really look at their faces, but I could already sense some gentle eyes locking onto me.

I said hi. I said I was drunk. I heard laughter. I said I was staying. The boys said something I don't know. Everyone left and I found out how shallow Buck was. I also heard the dumb surf jock say, "Buck got a home run."

"What's a home run?" I asked honestly. He didn't answer, and then Owen, another older party boy who always hit on but also looked out for me, and was also friends with Buck Henry, looked at me and then at the annoying surf jock.

"I don't think so," he said with a little sigh and a drink of his bottle of Coors Lite. I didn't know what the hell they were talking about, but all my confidence ran into my fake black tights. I stood in that kitchen and no girlfriends or ride, and now Owen was saying I wasn't even a home run. Sometimes life just sucks, I thought.

I realized the next time I saw The Fang that he had been the "Whoa!" at the party on the dirt mounds. I had remembered someone with huge dimples and gold tan skin and shiny locks of medium–length hair and a distinct stony voice. THAT was The Fang. Though he hadn't gone for it fully at that party, he knew he'd see me again. And he'd wait for me in the shadows patiently, like a panther.

The Fang, as we called him and only him, was a mix of Asian honey and Latino fire, and reminded me of the dudes in those Minoan frescoes. He was so different looking and perfect, like a model with chiseled white-guy features, soft brown hair, and almond–y eyes. There was an air of class about him, under his mechanic–by–day/roadie–by–night exterior. His smile was slow and sleek, every single time. And if a boy could be meek, he was that, too. The PDA's from him showed up in the middle of parties and intimate get–togethers with his friends and especially in Hollywood when we went to see bands. Everyone liked him, even with his black–black sinister eyes. ⚡

Between the time when I first kind of met him at the party and the night I really really met him, I had become the obsession of his friend, Carter, who was tall and cute as a package in an Angus Young kind of way. But piece by piece, he wasn't really that hot and he was kind of stupid. He and I kissed after a night at Toe's Tavern where the boys got us in because they knew everyone there. I had to pee after the bar closed. And even though The Fang was there, Carter walked me down to the grocery store, holding my hand. Before we got onto the market's asphalt parking lot, he moved me up onto a curb that bordered a dead–and–graveled garden. I was wobbly with my poofy bangs and favorite biker jacket and the heels of my steel–toe stilettos kept getting caught in my leggings somehow. The one I bought with the $265 I saved for a twin–fin surfboard. But I ended up getting grounded for an entire summer, so I bought the biker jacket instead.

I almost fell back when Carter slid his arms inside my jacket around my middle and kissed me. It was pretty good in a rocker roadie–ish way. Then he took my hand walked me inside the market. No one was there except for some half–asleep stoned stockboys. "Can you tell me if this sweet sweet girl can use the restroom?" The next thing I remembered was walking out of the market's back room down some bleached hallway to the stairs where Carter was waiting for me. When I got to the bottom, he said, "I think you need to kiss me again." He got my number. But he never called.

Some days later, we were all at another show, and someone told me Carter had a *girlfriend*. "What? What an asshole." But that didn't stop Carter from trying again, which also made it really easy for The Fang to swoop in and lock it down. We were at an afterparty at Carter's house because Ash loved Pritchard and had to follow him around everywhere. Pritchard played guitar and looked a lot like Kirk Hammett. Carter and The Fang roadied for his band. Ash drove. Of course we ended up back at Carter's big house waaaaay past the ghetto in the upper Dena Hills.

I had ignored Carter's looks all night. Ash, Ezze, Tess, and I hung out with the boys in the terraced backyard and then moved inside to the sunken rec' room. I think Carter's girlfriend was in the kitchen on the opposite side of the vintage hotel house. But that didn't matter. He was still pouting at me every time I looked his way. The Fang knew Carter's time was up. And honestly Carter knew The Fang was going to watch him sink and be right there by my side when I looked up. And he was smiling when I did look up. I had moved into a small crevice beneath the loft stairs in this 20–foot ceiling rec' room with a beer in hand, next to an old saloon piano. I sat on the Persian carpet, leaning back against some green leaf wall and crossed my ankles. Before I knew it, The Fang was next to me with a slick grin and a "Hi…"

I had to laugh.

"Hi," I answered. He had scooted down into a lazy slump, so his head rested on my shoulder. His body was perfectly proportioned, about 6 feet tall and totally fine. He reminded me of a laughing Buddha, and he always had the good bud. Supposedly the parties at his parents' place were amazing. "Have you been to one of their parties? They're insane and huuuge!" No. No. I was never invited even though almost everyone who knew us mutually assumed I had been to the house many times. I never had. I only saw the house once when this rich British slut named Oz (that I was friends with for like a week) and I ditched and went looking for the famous Fang House. I had his address when I called him one day from work to see if he wanted an invitation to our private end–of–ski–season sale. He said yes. I brought his address with me into Oz's black convertible Cabriolet with white leather interior and white canvas top. Her super HiFi stereo was blaring Betty Boo.

"Fuck, Ronnie. You keep hearing about it?"

"Yeah, everyone asks me the same fucking question—if I've been to one of The Fang's family parties yet. Oh! Turn here and just keep going up. It's at the end, in the hills up there," I motioned to the line through the dark smog.

"So, you've never been? Ever?"

"Nope. I don't know. It's kind of weird..."

"Fuck..." We slowed down. "Holy shit, Ron! Look!" I looked over at the massive arched metal gate with painted tile walls that read "Casa des *Fang*." Through the bars, we could see a huge Spanish style mansion on rolling knoll, a couple of tennis courts, and a mini version of the mansion past that. My heart raced, and I told her to get the fuck out of there before someone saw us. Seeing his house in person that day made me feel really weird and uncomfortable for some reason.

Then Carter lunged down at me. I think his girlfriend, who was a lot older than me and kind of looked like the girl in the Billy Idol video for *White Wedding*, was still in the kitchen. "Come here," he said in a demanding pant. "I want to tell you something."

"WHAT do you need to tell me?" I was acting pissed, but really deep down inside I was loving it. My arms were crossed and I rolled my eyes and looked at The Fang, who was still smiling at me. And acting like nothing else was going on.

"Can't I fucking tell you something? Can't I fucking tell you something? FUCK!" Carter was wobbling aggressively down at me. I knew he was embarrassed, and pissed. And he knew something had started between The Fang and me.

"OKAY!" I said. "Tell me something!"

Carter pulled my arm and leaned in so he could reach my ear, but my gut said it never mattered and it didn't matter anymore, so I pushed him back off me. He lost his balance and threw me tantrummed looks of disappointment. And even though his girlfriend was *still* in the house, he started to shout louder, "Fuck! I like you! Okay? I fucking like you!" He took a chance at the last minute, but it was too late.

The Fang locked his arm through my elbow and folded his fingers together and nestled his head on my shoulder again and said something stony and then rolled a joint that we shared. Then I got up and walked to the bathroom, shooting a quick "Hi" to Carter's tough girlfriend on the way. I don't know but she looked oblivious to the things he did and the way he was.

I ran into the bathroom, spewing alcohol vomit all over the mirrors and walls. I think the bile was a translucent nuclear green. Then I stumbled out, walked slowly to the sunken room and fell onto the mushy couch. I was still drunk and a little high. In a foggy minute, The Fang was lying next to me. He didn't really move, but it was the first time he tried to steal a kiss. I acted like I was asleep. He made sure his lips were close enough that a couple of times they touched mine. I would have probably scammed with him if everyone hadn't been passed out all around us, and maybe if I hadn't puked green bile a while ago. Carter was sitting at the top of the stairs. From the slits of my smudgy mascara eyes, I could see him shaking his head. Defeated.

A block of time passed between stealing pukey kisses and the two of us actually scamming. Carter was relentless, though, and of course he thought he could still win me back or dupe me. A few weeks later, we had gone to a party and then ended up at a get–together with the boys at one of their skater friend's houses in the Dena Hills. Like a lot of skaters, this random friend had a clowny appearance with tiny Ronald McDonald curls and different color tube socks scrunched down on each shin under long shorts and was really *spacey*. But I knew it was an act. He wasn't Pro. Maybe he wasn't aware that a lot of famous skaters were our friends. It just didn't fly.

So many Sketchwood skate rats grazed covers of *Thrasher* or showed up in Tom Petty music videos and Rice Krispies TV commercials, and of course all of them were getting laid. So we were unfazed by the notion that someone was a Pro skater because, in our town, who *wasn't* Pro? And really, who *didn't* skate? Their random friend thought himself a badass skater but was more of a music tech dude for the band The Fang and his friends roadied for.

We showed up just in time—not too many people and definitely not a lot of girls were there yet. It was a little chilly, with sporadic gusts blowing up from the mouth of this little valley.

Ash pulled up fast. She was so drunk. She lipglossed and brushed her hair and slammed on the brakes in front of the house right by all the cars parked. I was happy she was done maneuvering through these winding streets.

"There's Pritchard's car. There's The Fang's mustang. There's Carter's party Pinto." Yes, Carter cruised his tall motherfucker self in a brown Pinto with an orange racing stripe. All the boys and their big hair piled in that toy car. But it never hurt their image. It only made them look like they were totally serious about partying...and pot.

The front of the house was modern and sterile, parentless without any windows. Inside it was minimal and rich and the view from the backyard was insane. His house was atop the side of a cliff that overlooked The Rose Bowl with a small vineyard growing down the hillside. There was a huge fire pit and a very large half pipe close enough to the cliff's edge. Tonight the bonfire was burning and some boys were riding the scenic half pipe or clipping the tree behind it to get on top of the ramp.

Then Ash disappeared—most likely she had pummeled any girl lingering near Pritchard and was quickly climbing on top of his face. Ezze stood next to me. She knew how I'd be nervous to see The Fang and that sometimes I felt wobbly even before I'd had anything to drink in my chartreuse rayon jacket with thin black chevron lines, black leggings, and stiletto pumps. Ezze was wearing her fuzzy angora royal blue sweater that was so long she wore it as a dress. It kept falling off her shoulders, which she loved. She started to fuss with her bangs, which meant she was feeling insecure. But she normally had so much confidence even though she wasn't as pretty as her best friend Sydney and those obvious cheerleader looks. Even though her mind was on other things, she still watched over me and made sure I felt confident, especially when I was dead silent.

"One of the boys will smoke you out. Don't worry. Do I look okay, babe?" I could never understand or keep track of her unrequited crushes, except for Taylor's older brother, who was nice and good looking, in a very Shawn Cassidy meets Rob Lowe way. And he always had a girlfriend (that we never saw) anyway. I really think he loved Ezze. And I know she loved it when he was fucking her. But he wasn't here at the party. No. There was someone else that she had her seductive eye on tonight. I had no idea who it was, though, and I was too nervous to care. Carter was here. And so was The Fang. And I hadn't seen either one since the puking/yelling afterparty at Carter's and midterm exams. I knew it was going to be an interesting night.

"Come with me," Ezze gently lead me through the very beige halls into one of the full–wall mirrored bathrooms. It felt a lot like a hotel in Vegas.

"Why are you acting so weird?" I finally asked Ezze.

"No, doll baby," she smiled. "I just need to get laid." She was half joking and most likely making light of the night in case he rejected her affections. "Give me a kiss." I gave her the sweet tiny peck and we left Vegas. I started to feel great.

We walked around the round marbled sunken living room and past the sliding glass doors into the twinkly cool night. We saw the red glow of hot wood and walked over to the fire. Then I felt a presence in the darkness approaching me, facing me, then wrapping its arms around me.

"Are you cold?" A slick voice asked in the darkness. I looked up as the cinders sparked and popped in the fire pit. He was in his fitted black leather jacket which looked perfectly molded to his lean body and underneath was a perfectly thin worn navy T–shirt that fit his perfectly cut chest and defined shoulders below his chin length fade. And of course his jeans fit him perfectly. I didn't move as he ran his warm hands up and down from my shoulders to my wrists and up again.

"A little," I said nervously. Everyone else had faded into the darkness and all I could see were the lights from houses on the hills across the bowl, the moon, and the warm reddish nimbus above the pit.

"Want to go up there?" He kept his hands on me and pointed with his chin to the top of the half pipe where some people were sitting and drinking. I didn't know where the girls were or Pritchard or anyone. But I could sense Carter pouting behind me. The Fang acted like no one was there, but I'm pretty sure he was sending a message: dude–I–know–you–like–her–but–fuck–off–cause–I–like–her–and–she's–too–good–to–let–you–fuck–around–with–her way. It felt rad.

"I tried to get up there, but I couldn't climb that tree with my heels," I said to him. I could clearly see his face now, and fuck, he was beautiful to look at. Perfection. Just looking at him made my nipples gnar and tingle.

"Wait, I'll go up there and pull you up." With that, The Fang disappeared behind the huge skate ramp and reappeared less than a minute later in his perfectly fitting leather jacket and perfect brown skin and perfect hair at the top. He walked over to an open space and leaned down. "Here," he said, reaching one hand to me. I stood on the bottom of the ramp, trying to reach up, but he was too high, even with my 4–inch heels. I was about to fall when someone wrapped their arms around my hips from behind and pushed me up, with my legs floundering, until The Fang grabbed my wrists and pulled me up.

I straightened up and looked down. I saw Carter looking up at me and then at The Fang and then back at me, like a lost kitten, maybe realizing what he had just done. The Fang sat us down immediately before anything happened. Our legs dangling over the half–pipe, I could see everything clearly now. The girls, the band boys, the smokers behind the tree, and the lights from the Rose Bowl. And everything had a little hot glow. The Fang wrapped his right arm around my back and pulled me so I was crushed against his side. Then his right cheek was on my left cheek. We gently talked about everything, almost.

"Look at him," I said, looking down at Carter who, at this point, was standing at the bottom of the ramp, staring up at me, at us, with the most victimized look on his face. He wasn't really that hot to me anymore. I knew he was pissed because he couldn't start shit with The Fang. He just didn't have the right to. And everyone adored The Fang. So he was really fucked.

"Yeah," The Fang answered. But he could have cared less because right then, he turned slowly, his cheek still touching mine, then he kissed…my cheek. Okay, maybe I had to give him another try. By this time all of our friends were watching and I'm sure they were making their play–by–play comments. But I knew they were rooting for us. For me.

"Yeah, Carter's so dumb. Why does he act like that?"

"Yeeaaaah," The Fang answered in his elongated way, slowly turning his face toward mine again, still touching my cheek to his cheek. He had also pulled me closer to him, if that was possible, so we were a huddled bundle atop the skateboard ramp mountainside. But this time he locked onto my mouth and was pressing his perfect lips on mine, and pushing me hard enough that I had to lean back. I slowly opened my eyes a little and saw his eyes opened a little. The Fang smiled and I think I smiled, still kissing him. Then I closed my eyes again and it got firm and so good it was ridiculous. And somewhere in that goodness I heard him whisper "I know you." I didn't stop, and he never said it again. But I heard it.

We finally let go and smiled and I looked down to see Carter doing what he had done at the pukey afterparty in his parents' house—the "How could you?" pout.

"What is he doing?" I whispered.

"I don't know," The Fang whispered back, "and I don't care." And then he kissed me again. ⚡

The next day I stalled a little so I'd be tardy at school and have to get a slip from the office. If you were 18, you could write your own notes. I wasn't 18 yet, but I was so good at parental forgeries. And it helped that the people in the office knew I was a good student, even if they were all red–necky and prejudiced.

"Are you going to be late?" my dad asked, staring forward into his other–life fantasies or else other–life past memories, both of which didn't really involve us. I had been a daddy's girl up until I turned into a teen. At that point, the rules from his life didn't really work with mine anymore.

"I'll try to run. Bye, Baba." I kissed him on the cheek, got out of the little sun–roofed Beamer and stepped into the circle at the front of the main hall. I slowly slowly walked down the hallway toward the office until I heard the Beamer pull away. Everyone was in class already; I don't know why he didn't realize that because the main floor was dead empty. Partially due to it being a soggy morning. A lot of kids blew Fridays off, too, like they were in college or something which caused some teachers to give their exams on Fridays. Not that it did any good. You just can't sway a ditcher.

Anyway, I moved toward the office windows where I had to get a re–admittance slip for my "absence" the day before. But most of my friends worked in the office in the morning for credit, where they became a pet and could get a re–admit slip no sweat, or else they had worked in the office in the past and had a stash of blank slips waiting for us in their lockers. They also used to sell them or even trade them for a hit of green acid.

I walked up to the window, slowly, like someone who'd received a series of blows to the back of the ankles, hoping a familiar face would pop up. No one. Well, no familiar face that I liked. The Office Hags had made a living out of busting us. When really they should have made a living *saving* us. You'd see them huddled over their cheap computer system—which was plastic beige like all their other plastic beige crap that reeked of really bad synthetic carpet and old vacuum smell. I never got why people like the Office Hags existed. I. Hated. Them.

Really. I hated them that much. ⚡

The office reeked of a lot of things. It was dingy, trapped, too cold or else too hot, stinky, dusty, full of mites, uninspired. You'd walk up to one of three windows, fastfood drive–thru style, and subject your eyes to a space that was bordered on the inside by wood–paneled cubbies and clanky cold desks. The metal painted a faded mix of green and beige and yellow. The same color as bile. The same color as a lot of things I hated. The same color as a lot of things that were wrong. One day, forty years ago, they had been shiny and tan. Now they were as dirty as the yellow–y vinyl seats they sat their fat asses on. And that smelled of old carpet and used vacuum bags. But these Hags fit in perfectly, 'cause they sucked just as hard.

The Queen Hag had that hair I never understood, not even my gorgeous Lucille Ball bottle–redhead grandmother would dare have hair like that. It was ratty, on purpose, and trimmed exactly like the pubic hedges that lined most of the Hoity Toity concrete driveways. Furry birds' nests and old plastic grass. It, too, was a very light dingy metallic ash that smelled of Ogilvie home perm and old lady hairspray that comes out of white plastic spritz bottles. Her face was prune–y, like the stick up her ass was so old, it had left an unforgiving look on her face that drove her round–bellied husband to stick his hot dog into a lot of younger, non–sandpapery holes around town. It was written all over her periwinkle blues and barely–there lashes every time she looked down at you. She never believed that crusty stick would get stuck one day, but it did. Her hair and clothes and sex life were all stuck there, too. 1959 was the last time she ever looked fine. She was without a doubt how misery looks in horrendous clothes: polyester two–piece suits in dingy mustard and dry–poo mini–houndstooth and a wrinkled pert. The top was actually a vest that was sewn to the mock turtleneck. I didn't even want to think about the lingerie she was wearing. Her counterpart was the P.E. Hag who double–dutied in the office early in the day just so she could bust the people who ditched her awful drill–sergeant gym classes. "I see you and I'm going to check if you're supposed to be in class right now!" she'd shout on her way to the office if she saw anyone walking in the halls. She was totally butch in a very Helga way, a very square and kind of massive "woman," with gray skunk–striped hair that was perfectly parted in the center of her skull and petroleumed back, and painfully twisted into two pinned buns just behind her ears. Of course she wore no makeup under those tiny, wired eyeglasses that sat at the tip of her pointy nose. Her uniform consisted of white men's crew neck Tees, size XXL, dingy blue doctor's smock things, and old fitted sweatpants. And she always wore navy Keds. She was so strange in a horror movie kind of way.

She sat her fat ass on a stool, next to the Queen Hag, going over the attendance of some poor soul who'd be called into doom by a measly pink slip. You knew if you were sitting in class, and someone like the Twinkie Twins or the DeeDee's handed the teacher a pink slip, that it was probably going to be for you. But you hoped that it wasn't. So many people ditched that it wasn't that big a deal anymore. But there were still some poor souls who hadn't learned how to beat the system. It sucked for them. Because the Hags always sent those fucking slips.

Today the Queen Hag and Helga the P.E. Hag were mumbling over the computer screen at someone's schedule. They turned to glare at me with their opossum eyes and it made me nervous. Then I relaxed because they *always* looked like that!

The third Hag, and the one who came to my window, looked like a really bad hooker, with brassy flipped hair that was a little over–processed. She wore tons of foundation the way a lot of people did—a partly orangey beige coat that got a little Day–Glo and crusty on the edges just below the chin and next to the temples as the day went along. You could easily see it glowing from 30 feet away. She wore very late '70s dark sunglasses with a gradient amber tint, but it didn't hide the GOBS and GOBS of roller disco tricolor eyeshadow—*at 9:30 am*. One triangle of dark mushroom gray brown, one triangle of charcoal brown, and one stream of copper. Her lips were lined with dark chocolate and the center was glistening some strange salmon–y mauve color that was two shades too light, like the colors in those gift–with–purchase freebies at the mall. I thought it was maybe like the surprise cookies at Fredericko's; like they just mixed all the discontinued lipsticks together and gave it away.

She reminded me a lot of Lonnie Anderson on WKRP Cincinnati with her angora sweaters and lip–grip jeans. I still thought she sucked, though…'cause all she wanted to do was bust us, too.

"I need a slip," I said in my most innocent voice, though I always thought everyone in the office looking out at me was thinking the same thing—look at all her low class purple bruises.

I looked down at the concrete sidewalk. I felt like a dwarf when normally my 5–foot–3–inch self could feel really tall. I slid the note (that I forged on a bench around the corner) to her. It was a toss up. You just hoped you'd stepped up to the right window and be home free.

In my handwriting (because it was a fact and known that many kids wrote their notes in the car on the way to school and then had their parents sign the bottom):

PLEASE EXCUSE FARRAH KAZEROONI FOR BEING TARDY
TODAY AND FOR BEING ABSENT ON THURSDAY. SHE
WAS ILL.

SINCERELY, *Mr Kazerooni*

I signed my father's name because his English handwriting was terrible
and messy and I'm not sure if handwriting in his own language
was equally bad, but I signed it because it always worked. I had
been forging these notes for a year now. I started it at the end of
sophomore year. So I felt pretty confident because, at this point,
they had seen my forgeries so many times, they thought it was my
father's actual signature. But today, the Hooker Hag needed a bust.
The Queen and Helga had tallied up their busts that morning and
they were ahead, having one–upped the Hooker. And even though
they played on the same team, they'd even bust each other. Which
made me hate them even more.

The fucked thing was the Hooker Hag tried to act like she had your
back by tagging on something like Big Dot's "babe."

"I need to call your dad and confirm his signature. Okay, *BABE*? Can
I call him at home or is he at work?"

"Yeah, I think he'll be there." I was worried. More about disappointing
my dad who thought I was perfect than getting caught with a lie. I
stood there, trying to act calm, until she came back from her plastic
beige phone call. I felt like I might vomit for a second. I had issues in
the office. I guess that's why I always felt like they looked down on me.
A while back, someone had called and told these Office Hags that my
mother had been in an accident and was in the hospital and to have
me waiting at "the circle" in front of the main floor so they could pick
me up. The Office Hags had told the caller that they knew my father's
voice and that "this is not her father." The caller hung up. The Office
Hags had called my dad who came to school in a full–suspecting rage.
We stood there in front of these bitches as they all believed…that I
was lying. Even though I was crying and scared. At some point, I
lashed out at the Hags and they watched my father slap me on my left

cheekbone. I screamed, "See what you did! See what you did!" Then they looked back at their stupid computer screens, and the Hooker Hag peered from over her tinted glasses down her pointy nose and up at me. "Well," she said. "I still have to get you a truant." No one ever looked further into the fake call or took it seriously. Except for me.

"Okay," The Hooker Hag said as she filled out my re–admit slip. "He said it's OK, but he wants you to call him at work." There. I was dead. Again. No straight A's could save me, and, well, I didn't have them right now anyway. And they never really saved me before. Nothing could really save me. I walked inside and called my dad on the plastic beige rotary phone.

"Hi, Pop."

"Ronnie, why did they say the note was for an absence yesterday?"

"BecauseIwasreallylate,soIneededanotetoexcuseitasanabsencebe causeitwasmorethan10minuteslateandwhenyou'remorethan10 minuteslateitcountsasatruant." I froze for a second.

"Okay. See you later."

"Okay. Bye."

Fucking Hags. ⚡

I took my slip without a thank you and turned toward the main floor. I was already more–or–less 30 minutes late to my first class, French, which was really easy because I already knew three languages and I had studied French since the 7th grade. I decided to make my way down the vacant main floor toward class in case I felt like dropping in and getting the daily lesson. The morning was calm and cool like my blue polka dot ESPRIT shirt, white diagonal belt, white leggings, and favorite cream lace-up boots. But somewhere between B and H hall, I got lost in my head or something. The sunlight found a way to twinkle into dots on the grass by the snack area and off and on there were light shadows and prisms that crept onto the metal lockers and cold cracked concrete hall. And you'd notice the secret spots with everyone in class and everything was empty. These spots behind the benches where the boys' bathrooms were (they alternated boy–girl–boy–girl from hall to hall) and the shrubs between them on the backside of the main floor, where no one ever walks. Lots of supposed drug deals and affairs happened behind the bushes in those secret spots.

I finally woke from my haze and decided to waste the rest of the period in the last bathroom and then go see Mr. LeGrady to get the test review questions, because I had missed his modern poetry class the day before.

I walked into the girls' bathroom in H–hall. Taylor came out of a stall. Her giant dolly eyes and perfectly–separated almost–fake lashes blinked a big, slow, exaggerated blink only to open wider with a "Hi, Ronnie!" bright toothy smile.

"Hi," I quietly walked over to the mirror in front of the stalls. The bathrooms looked just like prison bathrooms in movies. They were ancient compared to the bathrooms in the invisible hall, which were newer and nice and dark. Sometimes I'd ditch in those newer bathrooms because you didn't *ever* get busted there. But you'd be alone, which sucked. Chronic ditchers always ended up in one of the last bathrooms on the main floor, 'cause you always knew *someone* would be in there. I bonded with a lot of people while I was blowing off class. It was other–worldly and social for sure. You were still a sitting duck, but I guess it was worth the risk. I only hid in those nicer bathrooms when I really just wanted to be alone.

But these bathrooms were bright peel–y white and beige thick chipped paint and empty metal tampon holders and bathroom stall locks that never worked. Windows that cranked open diagonally and old sinks that either dripped out a drop of water at a time or else gushed out so hard that you'd end up wet.

Taylor walked up next to me and put her clear plastic makeup bag on the tiny old decrepit wood shelf under the mirror. She unzipped her bag and took out her Wet–N–Wild blush. She was proof that you didn't need Dior to look beautiful. And that you didn't need to care what anyone else thought.

"What are you doing, Ron? Are you late? Do you need a note? I have re–admit slips," she sang sweetly as she swept the blush cake with the flat square brush. Then she looked in the mirror and began to fan her cheek back and forth, even though there was already a dusty rose stripe on each side of her face.

"I already got one, but thanks." I took the huge Sebastian No. 9 can out of my canvas bag and spritzed my bangs. I loved the smell of Sebastian No. 9.

"Ronnie, can I use that?" Taylor asked as she put her square Wet–N–Wild brush down on top of the compact sitting on the narrow–ledged shelf.

I handed her the can and then I watched her short natural nails and tan fingers poke in and raise bits of her bleached mushroom rocker hair. It was already high and big and explosive. Then she sprayed all around her mushroom and handed the can back to me. We stood facing each other silently in the sticky fizz. ⚡

"I love how that smells."

"Yeah," I answered. Just as I started to put it away, Big Dot walked in.

"What's going on here, babe?" she asked me, motioning to Willy that it was safe to come in.

"I just got here," I said, handing her my re–admit slip. Thank God I always had proof when Big Dot showed up. Taylor had a thousand of them, so she never flinched. And all of the Office Hags loved her, because she had worked with them nearly every semester since 10th grade. And the dickhead principal, Mr. Pain, lusted for her. She could have gotten away with murder, but Taylor was a straight arrow. She really never did anything wrong.

"Here, I have one, too." Taylor smiled that slow smile and did that slow blink that doubled the size of her already huge Day–Glo blue eyes.

"Okay, well, you should still go to class. Okay, babe?" she interrupted herself and looked at Taylor. "That lipgloss looks gooooood. What is that, babe?"

"It's Wet–N–Wild Powdered Donut," Taylor offered with another slow crazy gaze. She could get away with it because she was *that* pretty. She definitely could have dated the jock stars and star quarterbacks and been the cheerleader lead. And I bet there would have been scandalous rumors about her, her hot quarterback boyfriends, and their "fruit days" when he'd shove bananas or strawberries up her ass and then eat them out. Yeah, rumors like that would have spread IF she was a cheerleader—but she wasn't. She did always go out with the star drummers with the perfect hair, like Tommy and other big Viking rockers. But she was pure Metal and no one dare fuck with her. *Especially* about fruit day.

"Okay," we both answered, pretending to pack up while the bell rang. Yea! Missed it! Then Big Dot and Willy laughed something inside–jokish and left.

"Repulsors' show this weekend?" Her eyes beamed.

"Yeah. I guess. And that other party."

"Are you going to see The Fang? Won't he be at that party?"

"Yeah, I guess." I didn't really know what was up with The Fang. He had called one day, talked about his "tomato plants" that he was growing on his parents estate, laughed his typical "heh–heh" laugh, and dropped his completely sideways I–want–to–see–you message: "Ronnie, there's a party on so–and–so streets tonight with five Speed

Metal bands." ⚡

"Next to that huge church?" I had replied, smiling, because I could tell he was smiling at the other end of the line, alone, in his room, trying not to admit he liked me. That he wanted to see me. Later he'd act like it was a coincidence that we were both at the party, but everyone would know the real story. The night would be fantastic and dreamy and real and all just a few weeks before the dance at "the happiest place on earth."

"Yeah, he'll probably be there," I told Taylor. I knew he would, but I had disconnected. It was easier to just be the quiet lonely one than the one who does the dance with The fucking Fang. The fucking dance. Fuck the dance. I never understood that dance. The boy would tell everyone he "liked" you and be clowny and flirty and do it for two or three months, and his friends would call you and confide in you and take your arm and look at you and say, "Ronnie, The Fang likes you." BULLSHIT. I never got it. If you showed something, the boys would start acting like they never said they liked you in the first place. If you ignored them, they hunted you down. I never knew when to let my guard down, and it always felt like the second I decided to was the second I felt terrible for ever doing so. It's just the worst and for the most part I'd rather walk solo than deal.

"Don't worry, Ronnie," Taylor sweetly consoled me. I had no idea what my face had done while going over that painful picture in my head. But Taylor could see something through me. "Don't worry. Here, I wrote you a note." She passed me a folded piece of lined paper. "I wrote it yesterday, but I didn't see you after class." ⚡

The note was two pages folded over and over itself until it was too thick to fold anymore. Some of the girls folded their notes in secret style ways so you'd have to open it correctly or else the paper would tear. But it's not like it would tear into a million pieces, so I never understood the point. Still, it was fun to fold the notes in tricky ways. And it was common for us to write each other notes even though we spent every school day, nights, and weekends together. I don't know. It was like a sign that your friendship was special or something. If you didn't write someone a note, they'd be like, "Why didn't you write me a note?" Then there were times you got notes from a girl you knew who was in the top popular five, with some of the bullshitty girls you acted like you were friends with but didn't give a true fuck about and thought they were jokes. But in between their baked potato–and–ketchup diet the one nice girl would say, "Oh, Ronnie! I wrote you a note!" and it's all hyper and sweet and you learn if they can spell. And they tell you all about their older boyfriends and how they cheated with their ex–girlfriends and how the ex–girlfriend is a "poodle" and "go fuck your poodle" and it ends with, "Thanks for being so sweet, Ronnie" and you write back during next period 'cause now you want it to continue. But then there are other people who never really write notes, until they die. And even then you have no idea what the notes said. I wonder sometimes if Lex Phlat ever wrote any notes to anyone.

Lex was sweet, sort of. I mean, she had a really low, soft, almost invisibly quiet voice. And even though she didn't try to be loud, her personality and reputation was massive. Or out of control, maybe. At the beginning of high school, she was thicker, but never fat. I used to always hear about how badly she wanted to be skinny. More than the other girls, if that was possible. We all did, but with her it was extreme. Even when we all ate pizza from Percico's and cheese dogs from Clare's Corn Dog Hut at the mall. Even in junior high, when a girl I was friends with named Ari just froze all her food. She froze *everything*. Just put everything in the freezer "for later." And by the time we hit junior high graduation, she looked like a sallow–eyed skeleton in pink strapless taffeta. So, yeah, everyone was obsessed with it. But they'd eventually give it up for Lita or those Strawberry Shortcake Good Humor bars from the vending machines at snack. But not Lex.

Lex was pretty enough, but no matter what she did or how thin she got or what boy liked her, she just couldn't ever…catch up.

I never really got to know her. But I knew one of Lex's childhood friends, Olly. Olly loved to dish. She would tell me everything. There were some strange unexplainables at Lex's house. Her older sister was a total jock star student legend and maybe Lex was just left in her dust.

Lex was medium height, with longer legs in proportion to the rest of her body, and pretty narrow hips. Maybe her parents were narcissists; maybe she was beaten over and over as a kid. Who knew? She just always had the most vacant look on her face. You never knew if she was happy because she looked bummed out...all the time. I think she liked pot. And all the girls I knew who came from her junior high by the tracks in the middle of town, including Olly, liked pot and always had a little sticky dense nugget to share with you because "the babysitter brings it over all the time."

But even though I really knew Olly well, somehow Lex and I could never connect. She never really looked at me when she spoke. Not even when I was talking directly to her. And if she did kind of look at you, it was very brief and fake and soft and dead at the same time. And there was NEVER any solid eye contact. She was totally soulless, I thought, in a really creepy way. Somehow somewhere something had to have happened to her over and over and over that made her eyes filter out the light and glass over like that. You never saw her in class, just around the hallways in her short shorts when everyone knew she had stopped eating. "She only drinks Diet Dr. Pepper," Olly had said in a concerned high, standing outside the snack cage one day. "And she rides her 10–speed everywhere. Look how skinny she is." Then there were rumors confirmed that she'd be Scott Surfer's date for the next dance. Maybe she thought he just wanted to fuck her. But I didn't think so. I think he might have really liked her, actually. It didn't matter. The stories kept coming.

There were the stories about some party at her house. Stories about boys standing in a line outside a bedroom. Lex standing in the doorway, half alive, holding a sheet up around her totally naked Diet Dr. Pepper body, a BFF broken heart charm around her neck. While her brother sat in the living room, lifeless, attached to a video game. The house was silent. Or there'd be other news about her disappearing and ending up in some random's backyard, barely alive, and waiting for her friends to pick her up. She was numb, from the inside out. Sometimes I think she didn't know how to fit in, because no matter how thin she got or how tan or how good her BJ was or who took her to what dance, no one really ever talked to her. No one ever really knew her. Maybe one or two of the childhood "friends" like Olly sort of did at one point, and that was always in passing, and full of stories from eons ago when they were like 7. Now they'd have a quick chat in the hallway on their way to some party or date, without ever inviting Lex to come along. I don't think anyone really thought Lex would *want* to come along. That's how she always looked, anyway.

Then over Christmas break, she did it. Lex hung herself. People ooooh–ed and aaaah–ed for a day and then continued to talk about her and then they up and forgot about her…again. She had always been invisible to them. But I wonder, if the weeks before Christmas break, if she ever wrote any notes to anyone. If they were written and never torn out of her binder and folded in some special way that would tear if they weren't opened the right way, and passed off during snack breaks or makeup chats in the bathroom.

HEY!

WHAT'S UP, BABY? I CAN'T WAIT TO PARTY WITH YOU THIS WEEKEND! WOOO–HOOOO! LET'S GET WASTED!

MAYBE I'LL GET LAID! (YOU KNOW I WILL! HAHA!)

TELL ME WHAT'S GOING ON? WHAT'S UP, BABY? WHAT'S UP WITH ME IS THAT I'M TIRED OF FEELING LIKE A FUCKING PIECE OF SHIT AND I'M GOING TO FUCKING HANG MYSELF AS A CHRISTMAS PRESENT TO THE ONES WHO FUCKED ME! WOOOOHOOO!

GOTTA JET! LUV YA! BFF!

XXX SEXY LEXY

Yeah. I never heard of anyone ever getting a note from Lex.

⚡Christelle "Ezze" Sunshine Barbazette was Ash's partner in crime, and, like I've said before, Sydney's best friend. She was also Tess's favorite most of the time, Taylor and Devon loved her, and even the Russian, Rasha Balzac (we just called "Rif"), sometimes followed her lead.

To me, Ezze was a watchful eye. Someone who loved me and took care of me and got me. She saw through me and rooted for me and always included me.

Ezze wore whatever she wanted to, not that trendy shit. And to me and a lot of other people, she looked like she was backstage at a Fleetwood Mac show in Phoenix, Arizona circa 1979. I truly believe if we were in that era, she would have held even more power. As it was, she came pretty close. She was the strongest of us and at the same time she was the weakest. Her heart was always broken, pretty much, and so she'd just get too fucked up to care. Ezze loved crystal, which was perfect, because her dad was a mustached redhead Irish badass narcotics officer for the LAPD. That little detail came in handy, especially when the fucking paddy wagon pulled up to bust us for breaking curfew all the fucking time. They'd call all of our last names, one by one: "Manning! Schoeffling! Kazerooni! Barbazette! Yorke! Balzac! Twist! Keene!" We had the drill down hard: quickly squeeze the beer bottles into the tight crevice of the backseat, light a couple cigarettes to mask the smell of spilled beer, and sit quietly like little angels. Sometimes if it got bad, Ezze would pull out her dad's business card and hold it nonchalantly below her chin, facing it toward the officer grilling us. It always got us off the hook because of some code cops had about busting a fellow officer's kid. Then they'd be gone and everyone's heartbeat would go back to normal. Sort of.

Ezze was meek. She never had to worry or try. She was ALWAYS included and even fought over. We never challenged her shotgun status and always gave her the last word on party plans, which ones we'd attend and which we'd avoid. If there was ever an example of someone beaming so much light that everyone wants to be near them, whether they have fake boobs or not or the best body or not or the right shoes or not, that even–the–richest–most–popular–most–vacant–girl–will–kiss–your–ass vibe, Ezze had it.

Ezze was the one who'd say, "Grab Ronnie two 40's," when we'd score booze at the liquor store in El Monty when the crazy Asian lady at Star Liquor was too paranoid to sell to us. It's Ezze's voice I'd hear five minutes after we walked into a party—"So–and–so is going to smoke you out in the back…" And she never failed me. I'd walk to the back of the party where there'd be a circle of longhairs and trenchcoat boys with Jesus–and–Mary–Chain cuts and stranger dudes you didn't know who sat in the corner of your English class and dropped *WHAT DO YOU KNOW ABOUT MARIJUANA?* pamphlets in front of your eyes while you were reading one day as they walked by your desk. They'd be named Fred, and in the back of the party with the circle of Heshers and hippies and skinheads and oddballs, like Fred, you got to ask why he did that, as you passed around pipes and joints and passed on hits of acid.

"I don't know. You just look like you smoke pot." ⚡

The stoners always knew I was coming over, they never judged or acted like dicks, and they were always happy to see me. I'd get high and listen and laugh and then thank them and walk away to look for Ezze.

There were a couple of times when I couldn't find her after looking around for a while. Eventually I caught her walking back into the party from God–knows–where with Tina, the rich anorexic overly–tanned nymphomaniac. I started to realize they almost always disappeared whenever I was smoking out. They looked serious enough and were holding hands for balance in their high heel pumps. I just glared at Ezze. I didn't care for Tina. Even a little bit. Tina was *super* rich, the richest next to Jonesy, a strange but likeable girl who had three nose jobs by the time we were sophomores which led the competitive Tina to talk sarcastically at snack: "She looks even more perfect now, even though her nose was already perfect when it was natural." Those girls had more than everything they could have ever wanted. Though somehow you just knew one of them would end up marrying a super ass spaceball jock, who'd end up working for her masquerading Mafioso dad, and she'd get so sick of her micro–managed fake life that, in her early 20's, she'd take a schleppy holiday job at Noddy's Department store where her meltdown would surface as a crazy affair with some random stockboy and lead to a quickie divorce with the jock. Jonesy did have class and was supposedly chaste, like me. Tina, on the other hand, had a really weird vibe and was such a show–off with her endless supply of cars and conquests that, no matter what, I couldn't really like her. She thought she had us all fooled because we really just played along. We knew if Tina could fuck our boyfriends, she would. And she wouldn't feel bad about it. Just *act* like she felt bad, until she offered to drive us around in her new black Porsche and lure Ezze off with her China White affections. She bribed everyone with the five or six or ten cars she owned. I couldn't keep track of the phony. I mean, the most you could hope to get out of a conversation with her was a muddle about how her gold Beamer was in the shop, so she'd have her black Beamer for us to cruise around in, or how she had seduced yet another girl's boyfriend and how they wanted to kick her ass. I wondered sometimes, without her cars and credit cards and closets of clothes and stacks of shoes and endless allowances and drugs, if she had any *real* friends.

That's why I knew she and Ezze were "secretly" doing crystal. And a lot of it. I never saw them do it and wasn't really worried about it at first. But the fact that Ezze kept it away from me made it clear that it wasn't too good a thing for me to know about, and that Ezze might have a big problem with it herself. There were a few times when we were getting ready to go out and Ezze'd almost gloat to us about losing 10 pounds because she hadn't had an appetite "for three days." We knew she had been riding around with Tina. I think it bothered Ash the most, for a lot of reasons. It didn't make us love Ezze less, and the girls didn't really discuss it too much in front of me, but I heard enough bits to know that Ezze had kind of a serious problem with that stuff and that, of course, Tina did, too. The problem seemed to be escalating, but there was no reasoning with them at this point. We whispered about it with our eyebrows behind their backs.

Ezze was a very washed–out blonde with washed–out lashes that she hated. She was powdery, dusty rose, and milk chocolate mascara that didn't show. I wished she wore black, though. She had the same distinct mouth as her siblings with an exaggerated puckered upper lip that not even braces could fix. Ezze had a lazy right eye when she got drunk, and she smiled more than ever–ever–EVER when her large braces finally came off. But I don't think anyone noticed as much as she wanted them to. Ezze wasn't poor, but she usually didn't have any money. I didn't know where her money went. And she didn't really ever work. She couldn't because it interfered with all of her social obligations. Even though Ezze suffered from a lot of change–of–hearts and wishful thoughts (her heart got broken what felt like every week) I rarely ever heard her complain about it. ⚡

She comforted me when my dad was on his way to haul my ass home one night. "Have you seen my daughter? Have you seen her? When I find her…" Like we lived in some village somewhere. The thought of my dad out looking for me made me want to chum my guts. I had taken refuge at Rif's after a weekend of parties. Ezze put me on her lap. "Don't worry. We'll save you if we have to. You are good, okay? Don't forget that." They all knew why I told my parents to fuck off. That I knew I'd get punished again and it'd be worse this time. That's pretty much the only reason why I milked it for as long as I could and stayed out all night. My freedom.

Ezze pointed out your bullshit and made you confess to everything you thought you could hide. She was also one of the guys with her brother's friends, so they told her everything and then you'd hear everything relayed back, including of their exaggerations and lies. If you only dry–humped, and she heard them say they ate you out, she'd definitely tell them to fuck off and still laugh and give you shit about it.

One time, we went to one of the famous parties at the house by the big old church in Dena, the same house The Fang asked me to meet him at before, the same house that always had the Speed Metal parties. I was with Ezze and some of her brother's friends who gave us a ride. I had my two Mickey's 40–ouncers; one was open and the other was about to be opened. I hadn't been home for days and was wearing someone's clothes. But fuck it. We were all staying at the Fortunas' house. We used to be there all the time, until every single girl from my clique, plus all the fringe girls, ostracized GiGi Fortuna from our party circle, leaving her to drag herself sadly from class to class. For years she had been Ezze's BFF, and I think GiGi was totally shocked when, out of the blue, she was cast aside *and* taunted at snack by her dear old friends. I even joined in a couple times. But I couldn't tell you why. And she just surrendered to it, which confused me. It's like she knew she couldn't win. Anyway, I think the clothes were hers. They worked even though they were a little big and not me. But now I was done with my first 40 and starting my second, so the fuzzy angora sweater belted at my hips diagonally over white leggings and I think my black pumps didn't really matter to me anymore. Nothing did.

My hair was big and the music was LOUD. And that's all that really mattered. I think five Speed Metal bands were getting ready to play in this backyard jungle of jeans and hair and beer. Amid all of it, I noticed this very tall, super lean Surf Punk who stood out. His skin was beach tan and his hair was a needle–straight towhead bowl. An asymmetrical bowl–cut parted on the left, that is. With long white bangs that swung over his right eye and wrapped around until they met the very short hair above his left ear. The bottom half of his head was so short and dark and the top was so light and long. His dimples were deep deep and his teeth were perfect. He didn't stand totally straight and he smiled a very shy smile. I was too drunk to think about what The Fang was doing or how my parents were probably on the phone with the cops—but hopefully they wouldn't be. I was so drunk and had gotten to a place where none of it mattered anymore—not the grades or the rules or the bullshit conditions always placed on me.

Here, tonight, it was Ezze and me, because the backyard was as full as five high schools in a pot. Hesher soup. We couldn't find anyone we really knew. So I kept drinking and banged my head to the music, loud loud and light speed fast, which I loved because it was so much like Punk. Which is also probably why Charles liked it. ⚡

"Are you really drinking that? It's half as big as you are," he said loudly with a little lean and a little smile. He had been watching the band, skateboard in hand, and eyeballing my drunken wobbles peripherally. "Are you really drinking that?" he shouted again.

I laughed and wobbled and pointed to a large bottle rolling around between heels and sneakers and boots and studs. "THAT WAS MINE, TOO!"

"What's your name?" His face was practically in mine because the music was so loud.

I was a wobble a syllable.

WAN–wobble–NA–wobble–HAVE–wobble–SOME?

He smiled. I was totally fucked up and everything looked black and thorny and chaotic. But in the mass static was this very still, very quiet, bright deviant. He was just like me. We loved Punk and Speed Metal parties at this famous party house by the old church in Dena, and it didn't matter if I was in someone else's foofy sweater or that he had blond skater hair. He got me. And I didn't have to do a thing.

"WAIT—WHAT'S YOUR NAME?" He shouted again.

"RON–NEEE—"

"RON–NIE?"

"YES! WHAT'S YOURS?"

"CHAR–RLES—"

I shared my second Mickey's with him. After what felt like forever, in a good way, Ezze emerged from the dark thorny mess.

"CHAR–RLES—" I shouted to her face, pointing to the tall figure smiling down at us.

"Ohhh," Ezze said under her breath just like Mae West. That sobered me up a little. He must really be a fox, I thought. "The cops are here. Come on. We have to go. Give him your 40, babe." She took my hand, I smiled up at him and got quickly pulled away into the barely lit avenue. I felt sad that it was done and I'd probably never see that hot beanstalk again. All because of the fucking cops.

Just as we approached her brother's van, Ezze pointed across the street. "Ron, there's your towhead over there."

"CHAR–ULLLZZZ!"

He turned, caught me, and called back.

"WHAT'S YOUR NUUMMM–BER?"

"YOU WON'T REMEM–BERRR!"

"WHAT'S YOURRRR NUUMMMM–BER?"

"FOUR–FOUR–FIVE–TWO–EIGHT–EIGHT–NINE!"

"I'LLL CALLL YOOOO!" he yelled. Even from way across the darkish street, I could see his amazing smile.

The muscles in my cheeks hurt.

"*Mmmmm–hmmmm*," Ezze hummed with that mama bear look in her eyes.

The next day, because of Ezze, all the girls knew about the Surf Punk babe. Even in the moments with 300 drunk Heshers pounding their heads to gloriously mind–crushing Speed Metal, Ezze was awake to my every move. Ezze and I had something between us that I valued and could never explain to anyone. Not that I tried. We named this connection "The Third Life" one of the times I ran away from home and was hiding out at Ezze's house.

Ezze's younger sister, Winnie, loved it when I was over. She was a miniature version of average–sized Ezze, with enormous aquamarine eyes and dirty blonde hair. She shared the same father as Ezze and their older brother, but Ezze's stepmom was Winnie's real mother. So Winnie kind of ruled the house. "Want to hear my new song?" she'd ask me whenever I was around which, at this point, was a lot. It was pretty clear no one really took her seriously. But I loved to hear everything, especially because Winnie loved Metal and practiced her drumming incessantly. She worshipped Rick Allen and Sandy West (which made me love her more) and had a collection of porcelain lamb figurines in her very light yellow room that looked more like a rock nursery with its green glitter and chrome miniature drum set that sat right in the middle. She was a determined little thing no matter if anyone cared or not. "What are you playing for me?" I asked, sitting on her kiddy bed. She sat on her stool, looked at me calmly, and said, "*Lovers.*" ⚡

In between toast and jelly and eggs, her nark dad and stepmom offering to adopt me and sister venting to me about 7th grade woes, Ezze and I found ourselves lying on our backs, side by side, with the bottom of our feet pressed against the wall in the tiny hallway between her bedroom and the kitchen. Everything I started to say was finished by her. Every song we started to sing, we sang at the same time. I would have stayed in that hallway on the floor with Ezze forever with our feet pressed up against the wall, her family hopping over us like nothing was wrong. Like it was just a normal day.

Even though that time I had practically moved in, I couldn't tell you what her room looked like, what color her bedspread was, whose picture was under her pillow, or what drawer she kept her panties in. But I knew that hallway. On that hot and hungover afternoon, the hallway was serene, calm, cloudy, quiet, and safe. Ezze gave that to me.

Without my ever asking for it. And the best part was I didn't owe her anything. I always wanted that time in the hallway to happen again, but we never really got a chance to go back. Everything sped up. So I just signed notes to her as "The Third Life" and left it at that.

I don't know how many of her "friends" and followers and fanatics ever saw her crack. I hardly ever did. Once in a while, you'd catch her standing there in mid–hair–fix motion, without the smallest look of disdain or anger or sadness on her face. Just a bit of a smile. Where the top teeth sit on top of the bottom teeth, perfectly. But you knew about the tears painfully lodged in the back of her throat because they'd show up in her voice. And she'd use all her might to keep them way back there. It was usually because of one of two dudes and sometimes both at once.

The first affair was just pure fun and didn't last into junior year because he got really fat and she got prettier. He was the guitarist of a Punk–Metal joke we loved called The Repulsors. One of the Tommy's was their official drummer (and Taylor's man). There were lots of nights after a Repulsor party where Ezze would disappear with their lead guitarist dude, Coxxo. That was pretty much the only time when anyone'd see her totally crippled and, well, exposed. I never understood the appeal of Coxxo. She was too cute and smart for him. Maybe he fucked her really hard or maybe Ezze was the one who was good in bed. I never asked Ezze about it, and I'm not sure anyone else ever did.

⚡ Then there was Taylor's brother, Denny. He was a tiny bit older and playful and pretty in a very Robbie Benson way. Their parents were old hippies who lived just north of Sketchwood in a little tree house from the late '60s in a place everyone called Munchkinland, because all the houses were so storybook looking. The hilltop house was brown with orange lights and hanging spider plants: mushroom clocks and ashtrays, old cookbooks and owl–shaped incense burners. And under a table, Taylor's Muppet Guinea pigs, Roth and Chopi.

I know Taylor and Denny hated their house and everything in it, but we loved it. Especially the view from Taylor's very clean crystal white bedroom on the almost–top branch. I never saw Denny's room, but Ezze had, many times, and we heard it was all about blacklight THOR posters. Denny cared about Ezze and was close to his sister and was a good guy all around who wasn't too concerned with his big blue eyes or his perfect Hesher hair. The same hair you see on rocker babes in really old issues of Tiger Beat. But I think, deep down somewhere, Ezze properly rued the day she and Denny hooked up first. He was sweet and addicting and probably a dream between the sheets.

This one night, we were at a small party at some big vacant house in the Sketchwood hills. I was sitting on the back porch with one patio lamp and the warm moonlight on my face.

"Hey, Ron, wanna get high?" He asked me with the same enthusiasm as a little league coach.

"Yeah." We pulled two patio chairs together, one for me and one for Denny.

We hit the pipe a couple of times. Denny looked straight up into the moonlight. "Pack another bowl," I said.

Denny looked at me and grinned, "Fuck! I'm so stoned! How can you not be high?!"

"One more," I said smiling. When I was sitting outside with friends on a warm night, and nice dudes were telling me stories and smoking me out with KGB, for me it was even better than the sex I wasn't having.

"Fu–u–u–u–u–ck!" He packed one more sticky bowl and passed the sneak–a–toke. It was a little wooden Tiki head with the word WOWIE on it. I pulled it so hard, I started choking while huge popcorn puffs trailed out and up into the porch light. Then I passed it back. He pulled it hard, shutting his eyes tight for as long as he could hold it in.

"Another one," I just wanted to sit in the warm air in the big vacant back porch under the big vacant night.

"Fuck, DUUUDE! How can you not be stoned!"

"Another one!" So he packed another bowl. That was the type of guy Denny was. He would sit in the dark and repack a bowl over and over with his own pot when he could have easily been inside with girls sucking his dick, maybe even Ezze. Though I'm not sure she really did that, the blowjob–with–braces thing.

Ezze loved Denny, and we let her love him. We understood even though he never fully gave himself to her. He only gave her enough to keep her *there*. And I guess that was enough for her, because she always made it sound like everything would be alright.

Like, with the braces thing. She'd just give us a little smile and say, "You just have to be reeeeaaaallll careful." ⚡

Star light

Star bright

First star I see tonight.

I wish I may

I wish I might

Have the wish I wish

Tonight…

I made my way out of the ditchers' bathroom and stopped at my locker before going to see Mr. LeGrady during snack. No one was really in the hallway except for one very short (shorter than me) girl that was maybe a freshman or something with frizzy kinky hair and a somewhat very round frame. Her eyes beamed when she saw me. She called to me, "Ronnie! Ronnie!" like she fucking knew me. I stood there silently, watching her approach, until she stopped right in front of me. She delivered a message with a lot of white in her eyes: "Ronnie, Suzee is looking for you."

I stood there like Frankenstein. Then I replied in a very slow Dracula voice, "My name is Far–rah." The whites of her eyes got bigger and even though it felt a little bitchy, I didn't really care because I had to throw out a little message of my own.

"Oh." It was obvious she hadn't expected that kind of reaction. But the day hadn't even started, and any day where you had to deal with Office Hags AND bathroom busts AND classes you'd missed for days with no homework done AND the chance you'd have to take a test totally unprepared was going to draw out your inner bitch. Yep. The white–eyed sophomore continued with a lump in her throat so massive, it could easily be heard in the next mutter she dumped out. "Um, Suzee is looking for you."

She stood there looking at me, in her not–so–white T–shirt and mint green sweat pants. Where could she go?

"O–K," I answered and I turned back around to my locker.

She must have walked away, maybe in tears. Maybe she flipped me off first. I just didn't give a fuck. The bell rang and I knew I wouldn't find Suzee now. I had no idea what she wanted anyway because we hadn't been friends for two years, and her on–again–off–again manner was just a waste of my time. No matter how much we shared as kids, my gut said she was a pathological liar and manipulator whose convenient bladder infections got her out of ev–ery–thing. She hadn't worked a day in her very privileged life, and I figured out she had pursued and probably fucked any boy I had loved or was interested in and then played it off like nothing happened. Like it was all in my head. "We played solitaire all night," was her usual response. And I was happy she had never met The Fang.

So I just blew it off and made my way to Mr. LeGrady's classroom at the beginning of D Hall, just off the main floor.

Mr. LeGrady's Zen poetry class was another heaven, but we couldn't hang out in his class the way we did in Mrs. T.'s. Well, maybe we could have. But what would we do? Just sit in the back? Watts LeGrady was a total Beatnik with a short goatee and black lashes, white white skin and pretty short hair. He always wore black T–shirts and black jeans except when he wore black button–down wovens and a bolo tie made of braided black leather with a silver and turquoise feather fastener. And he always had black licorice on his desk. The twisted kind.

No matter who you were, he always remembered you. Not just your name and face, but everything, even though he seemed slow and stoned and bored off his ass with his foggy one-note voice. We all worshipped him and wondered how he could be the way he was in the world we lived in. He went to our shows and showed up in the back of our parties, holding a beer, supporting our bands. Sometimes he'd be reading alone in the back of the Country Kitchen coffee shop that looked like a windmill because it used to be a Van de Camps. I heard he always sat in the same booth and ordered his regular French toast with two strips of bacon. Even though he looked like he ate like a starving writer. Once, I ran into him at an ATM machine in Hollywood on The Strip. We were going to the same show. "Mr. LeGrady?"

"Yes, yes," he replied with as much enthusiasm as he could muster for a Beatnik poet who ended up in the middle of a bunch of spoiled brats and faculty who had sticks up their asses. "Far–rah, Far-rah Kaws–uh–roo–nee. You were in Modern Poetry your sophomore year. You sat in the second seat in the third row and you did your report on EE Cummings' poem 'your homecoming will be my homecoming', right?"

—when all fears hopes beliefs doubts disappear.
Everywhere and joy's perfect wholeness we're.

The dude remebered EVERYTHING! He was famous for it. And as long as you made an effort to get caught up in class and study sometimes and act like you were paying attention, he really never gave a fuck if you were truant or your re–admit slip was bullshit. He treated us like humans.

He was so different from everything at Sketchwood.

I walked into the emptyish room as the Twinkie Twins, who silently smiled at me, were leaving. I approached his desk quietly. Mr. LeGrady had his stony face on, as usual.

"Mr. LeGrady? Hi," I said gently as he looked up at me. I was nervous. I always felt like the teachers knew I was full of shit, and with him I actually felt guilty. "I have a re-admit slip, but I wanted to meet with you about the test review that I missed."

"Okay. Can you come back at lunch?" he said with his long drawl.

"Yes."

"Okay, then, Far–rah. Come back at lunch and we'll go over the test review questions you missed."

Okay, I said and left, leaving my anxiety at the door.

Everyone was already at snack and the gossip had already begun.

A muddle here, a muddle there. There were regular spots right off the main floor where the it–girls and mutt boys huddled—where they'd definitely be seen. The surfers were a ways down under their giant oak tree. The band geeks were far off from the main floor crowd, closer to the row of caged vending machines that offered my favorite strawberry shortcake Good Humor ice cream bars.

The popular snack treat was a big fat soft pretzel (that had been thawed that morning) and was handed to us by plastic–aproned, hairnet cafeteria hags. I made my way over to the pretzel line, scanning around for someone I knew. I hated snack and always wished I was sitting far away with the surfers and the oak tree.

I couldn't find Ash, who had probably decided to go home early and come pick us up later. She was 10 feet tall, so I always looked for her first. Then I finally spotted Sydney squeaking away as usual with Ezze. Tess was standing next to them, which meant that Tina had also decided to ditch. Probably to snort some crystal and plan the seduction of some poor girl's boyfriend. Her known Modus Operandi was to call them over to her single–level mansion, open the door in a g–string and wife beater with nothing underneath except her little mosquito titties and a quick invitation into her leopard bedding. She was so subtle.

I noticed Syd and Ezze talking to Jonesy. Jonesy was also a tanning–BJ junkie, and naturally born cute as a button. She was nice, but not the brightest. Ezze was touching the tip of Jonesy's nose as I walked over.

"Hi, little one," Ezze smiled and played with my hair. I could tell she was seething with news for me. Syd turned to squeak with someone else.

Then Ezze started, "Jonesy had another nose job."

"What? Again?" someone said in disbelief.

"Yes! Number four! But don't tell her I told you!"

About four girls had gotten nose jobs and maybe ten had gotten boob jobs at Sketchwood. The most I had ever done is go tanning. I had the scar from 22 stitches on the inner of my right arm, but that didn't count.

An annoying girl named Beatrice who tried to defect into our group from her Gothy clique had also gotten a little job on her Italian nose because she had "trouble breathing." Even though she was Italian, her real nose was pretty tiny. The job destroyed her near-perfect face, leaving the right nostril noticeably larger than the left.

"There's more!" Ezze whispered. "Cricket's in love with Johnny, but he's been ignoring her because she got so drunk last weekend she puked on him!" Cricket was the other Twinkie Twin and another fake blonde. It bugged me that she liked Johnny or Johnny considered her mole face attractive.

There was a time when Johnny and I weren't friends. But we got each other when we finally "met" one night. He was one of the surfers who hung out under the oak tree at snack and he also ran track. A purist with curly hair and crispy red Vans with clean laces who didn't really know me until one Halloween night when I was dressed like a baby and looking for my first asshole boyfriend at a football game. On my way to not finding him, I ran into his friends from the track team. "Did he blow you out?" one of them asked me. It was followed by some laughs and then Johnny said, "Just hang out with us." *Us* included Johnny's slut for the night, a girl I knew of even though she wasn't from Sketchwood. Much later that night, we ended up at Big Boy's. And when his slut finally left to use the restroom, I shook my head at Johnny like, "What the fuck are you doing with *that* girl?"

"I know! We should just leave!" Johnny laughed and I ate her French fries. I was still chewing when we pulled a dine–and–dash, leaving that girl with no money or ride.

Next week at school, I ran into Johnny on the main floor. But I was hesitant to say anything until I saw him wave.

"Hey!"

"Hey!" I waved back.

We were always friends after that. I must have had a secret crush on him, especially after we TP–ed his house. He never found out about the toilet paper, or my crush.

⚡Snack was bubbling with bullshit. Who broke up with whom. Who got new surgery. Whose BJ sucked. A place to show off new boobs, new dresses, and witness gnarly new hookups in the flesh. Most of the people at Sketchwood High lived for this shit. Like the DeeDee's. Especially the DeeDee's. Lots of DeeDee's who had lots of attitude because of their perky–boob DeeDee lives. One of them went too far when she recruited a totally unassuming geek named Peter Best and made him over into her personal mutt. He had always been extremely shy and soft spoken to the point where it was common to hear, "I never knew he existed!" But the DeeDee with the famous–but–strange perky boobs changed his hair and clothes and made him her mutty boyfriend overnight, which catapulted him straight into the popular scene's pisshole. All she had to do was parade him around with her perky boobs at snack for everyone to see. And PRESTO! Instant popularity! I mean, I got it...that it was a win–win for both of them. He got the fame and she got a pet. Before Peter, a lot of the mutts had already "dated" her. One mutt had bragged to the other mutts about fucking her at a party one night and leaving her in bed, and then fucking one of her friends right after in another room in the same house, then he had gone back to perky boob DeeDee and fucked her again. The thing was, she found out at some point and didn't even care. Or acted like she didn't care. Now she had Peter Best who stood by her like a trained poodle, with the same vacant stare as Lex Phlat. He even started riding a bike, a crotch rocket, at the DeeDee's suggestion because it "would help" his new Top Vomit image. Somewhere down the line, he'd crash and all her hard work would die with him. And everyone would secretly wonder if his senseless popularity makeover had been worth it.

"Hey, Ronnie," Olly was walking over to me with a little ball of tin foil. "My sister's babysitter left this for me, but I won't smoke it. You can have it, *if* you have any good stories for me." Olly was nice and sweet and had been friends with me ever since the Disneyland field trip, which was kind of her fault, sort of.

The big Disney trip for all three junior highs in Sketchwood. A huge mistake. The prissy crew from my preppy school in the foothills got mashed in a bus with other schools and the hardcore freaks on their roll call. Death rockers and the super Goths who wore black on their eyes, lips, cheeks, and nails, spiked their purple–black hair, smoked cloves, and actually smiled a lot for Goth kids. They sat in the back of the bus by Lex's old friends, Olly, Jamie, and Tin–Tin. I somehow ended up near the back of the bus, by Olly and those fiendish smiles. I didn't know what to expect, but I knew it was definitely going to be a trip.

First, the buses pulled off the freeway and stopped, and the chaperone moved passed me toward the cackling pack in the back.

"WE HAD TO STOP THE BUSES BECAUSE THE BUS DRIVER BEHIND US SAYS BOTTLES ARE HITTING HIS WINDOW! OK! YOU CAN'T BE DRINKING! AND YOU CAN'T THROW THINGS OUT THE WINDOW!"

It was quiet, but you could hear the inners of the Goth girls laughing so hard they were dying inside. And as soon the bus started back on its track, the Goth girls began singing in a cocky a capella of "Let's Go To Bed". I was sitting alone, kind of. None of my core friends were there, so I had tagged onto another threesome I sort of knew. But I felt totally excluded because no one was really talking to me. And I had no idea then that the reason why they weren't talking to me was because almost every single person on that bus had a bottle of something stashed between their legs. Then a girl with a million separated–with–a–safety–pin lashes tapped my shoulder from the seat behind me. That was Olly. "Do you want some?" handing me a bottle of Irish whiskey. After a while and a few swigs I was having such a blast that the awkward loneliness I felt had completely vanished. I was caught up in this party with my new friends until I felt someone in front of me tugging on the whiskey I was waving around. I tugged back, still laughing and rambling on to the new friends in the seat behind me who had suddenly become weirdly silent. The tugging got harder and I finally swung around and watched in slow motion as the chaperone tugged my first bottle of booze right out of my hand. I was too confused to understand what was actually happening. It was so fast—until he took me to the front of the bus.

They demanded the names of the girls who were drinking in back "or else." "I don't know any of them. They don't go to my school." The booze wasn't mine and I knew I'd be killed, but there was no way I was going to rat the girls out. "Okay then we'll have to tell your mother," even though I begged them not to. My lip popped open when she slapped me for embarrassing her. First liquor. First bust. And for months and months, my last night out.

When I started high school, I re–connected with the very same girls from the back of the bus. They were so friendly to me, fluttering around me like a dust devil storm. "You're the girl who didn't tell on us!" That's how I became allies with the Goth girls and Olly.

She handed me the babysitter stash. As I opened the foiled square, I got a waft of the sweetest stink I had ever smelled. "Wow–are you sure you want to give this to me?"

"Totally," she answered. "She brings it over every week." I held onto that hairy nugget for weeks and carried it around until one ditch day, while driving in Tina's gold Beamer, I finally decided we should smoke it. It was the last time I ever went back to class *that* high.

Olly threw her bag over her skinny shoulder. She was sweet and trustworthy, and I just knew she'd never change.

"I've got to get to class. Are you going to that Repulsors' party tonight?" Her fatigue–green eyes intensified.

"Yeah."

"Is The Fang going to be at the party?"

"I don't really know. I haven't heard from him," I said in trailing wonder.

"Well, I'll see you there." She gave me a hug and left snack. Just then Ezze floated over to me.

"Everyone's either going to Tommy's or somewhere else right now to get wasted. No one wants to stay at school today. Do you want to come or do you have to stay?"

Of course I was coming. "I have to get the fucking test review questions from Mr. LeGrady," I said, remembering. "I can't blow it off."

"We'll come back and get you in an hour. I'll make sure Ash picks you up." Ezze smiled and I skipped off to Mr. LeGrady's classroom.

I walked a little down the main floor past a huddle where Ash, Devon, Tessa, Tina, and Sydney were figuring out where we'd meet, who would be driving, and all the other who–who details of the night.

Tess called out, "Ronnie! Do you want to get your nails done?"

"Yeah!" I threw back over my shoulder. "I just talked to Ezze! I have to go see Mr. LeGrady!"

"Okay! We'll be back in 45 minutes!" Ash shouted over their heads. "Your little ass better be at the back door!"

"Later, Smegs!"
"Later, Smegmator!"

I rushed to Mr. LeGrady's classroom, even though I wished I had blown it off and escaped with the girls. ⚡ I walked into the linoleum classroom, where Mr. LeGrady was sitting at his desk, eating an apple, and reading a book called *Divan of Hafez*.

"Mr. LeGrady?" I asked softly, my head looking down a bit and my eyes cautiously looking at him. "Is there any way we could do the review now? My ride is picking me up in half an hour."

"Oh hi, Far–rah. Sure. Yes–yes. We can go ahead and begin the review. Why don't you sit there," pointing to a desk by his podium. Then he got up, slowly, and, slowly, walked to another desk, turning it to face mine. He was so slow. Like he wasn't running out of time. He finally sat down and crossed his hands on the desk, his shoulders somewhat shrunken, and began his elongated philosophical test review sop.

"Did you read the passage I passed out last time, Far–rah?"
"You mean…um…I don't think so."
He handed me one of the sheets on his desk.
"Read this and tell me what you think it means."
I sat there in the echo–y hollowness of cold tile and chalk:

…If the condition
of things which we were made for is not yet, what were any reality
which we can substitute? We will not be shipwrecked on a vain
reality. Shall we with pains erect a heaven of blue glass over
ourselves, though when it is done we shall be sure to gaze still at
the true ethereal heaven far above, as if the former were not?

"I don't know. I mean, is it about death?"

"Perhaps. What else do you think it means?"

"I don't know."

"Okay, well, take it home and study it. What about the other story we discussed?"

"Which story?"

"The flood story. The one about the religious man caught in the flood—what did that mean to you?"

"Um…God?" I saw a teeny smile. Probably the only one I'd ever seen.

"Study them. This one, too." He handed me another sheet. "You'll have to explain one of them for the test. What you really think they mean." Then he got up, without saying another word or looking at me, and went back to his book, his apple, and his head. "That's all," he said.

I grabbed my bag tightly and ran down the main floor to the back door. I could see the Big Red Bronco at the far end of the locker–laced concrete tunnel. Fuck. I hoped they hadn't been waiting long.

Devon was smiling at me through the limo tint. I opened the door and jumped onto the backseat, out of breath, next to Ezze. Ash was fucking with her stereo.

"Are we going to Tommy's?" I asked. None of the girls were drunk… yet. Devon was shotgun (the only person who could bump Ezze out of that spot), nibbling away on her teriyaki trail mix, which meant she was working out like a maniac and dieting again. She was a fitness addict, but she partied just as hard. A devoted Danzig fan and glamour freak who worshipped Chanel with me. I took a look at the sheet Mr. LeGrady had given me at the end of the review:

How do I love thee? Let me count the ways.
I love thee to the depth and breadth and height
My soul can reach, when feeling out of sight
For the ends of Being and ideal Grace.
I love thee to the level of every day's
Most quiet need, by sun and candlelight.
I love thee freely, as men strive for Right;
I love thee purely, as they turn from Praise.
I love with a passion put to use
In my old griefs, and with my childhood's faith.
I love thee with a love I seemed to lose
With my lost saints, I love thee with the breath,
Smiles, tears, of all my life! and, if God choose,
I shall but love thee better after death.

"Ronnie," Devon said with giddiness in her slightly crooked teeth. "We're going to Newcastle. We don't know how they found out, but the cops were already at Tommy's when we drove by." ⚡

We cruised in the perfect sunlight across town to Newcastle Park, which was small and tucked away on a backstreet. Not too many of the kids were there. Only the serious would drive across town to party in a park so early on a school day. Only the diehards.

It was nearly impossible to hide Ash's Big Red Bronco in the parking lot. She pulled into a spot as far away from the entrance as she could find. Then we slipped out and walked over a knoll to a rickety picnic table behind the racquetball courts.

"Where's the beer?" Devon asked in her thick rasp.

Ezze scanned the park. "I think Taylor and Eugene were bringing beer," she said. But after 20 minutes with no beer in site, the atmosphere deflated. I sat down next to Devon and reapplied my lipgloss. I noticed her investigating a narrow groove in the weathered tabletop.

"What–the–fuck," she said, fidgeting with a crack in the splintered wood. "Is that…a fucking roach? Check it out!" In between a tiny finger pinch was a wrapped bit that looked like a dirty cigarette butt. She looked at me, then at the roach, sniffed it, and laughed in delighted disbelief. The gods had spoken and we were listening. She looked at me, grinning with her Cuban hazels. "Dude! Let's smoke it!" We were stoked.

No one else would touch it. But Devon and I were happy to stick it in our mouths. We got *there* immediately, the sun pounding on our foreheads.

"I wonder who hid it like that…" I said, coughing.

"Oh well…" Dev started laughing again.

Then Ash got nervous. "I can't get busted by the cops for ditching," panic coating her voice. "My dad will fucking kill me and we won't have a car."

Devon smiled her crooked smile at me. She didn't give a shit about that stuff right now. I mean there's something about weed that your friends who don't smoke don't get. That you can bond for life over a good toke.

We made our way back to the Big Red Bronco in normal formation—Devon was shotgun, then the pecking order went to Ezze and then me because the other girls were usually with their boyfriends. I liked the back, anyway. We slid out just as a cop car pulled into the lot. Ash lit up a cigarette to mask the stale dooby stink that had followed us back into the car, just in case the cop wanted to bust us.

The nail place was only three blocks away. Ash parked and we all jumped out.

"How much are those little loop charms?" I asked.

"Three dollars," the girls answered in sync.

Le Nails was a phenom and its own cheesy strip mall world of scandal and money, with jingle bells on the door. The jing–a–ling was immediately followed by a rapid Asian accent: "You pick your cull–ah." Kim the owner sat in front of the salon, her blunt bob swaying as she rotated the one–pound dumbbells with her lazy 22–carat wrists. There were other nail shops, but everyone in Sketchwood went to Le Nails for their acrylics, and everything else. You could be sharing the same nail dryer with your biggest enemy and you'd just have to fake it until you were free.

The carpet was a scary mix of synthetic blue and acrylic dust twinkle, piled with tables in rows. Strange photos of hands holding roses with imitation dew drops on fake flower petals in cheap plastic silver frames were here and there on the walls. The clawlike nails in the pictures showcased speckled, airbrushed, and even weird Christmas designs.

Behind every table sat an Asian lady—some old, some young, some Korean, some Chinese. Which was also weird. I mean, when did fake nails become an Asian thing? They did their work, took the money, and handed it over (with tips) to Kim, their "master."

"You pick your cull–ah."

Her slaves were sweet and charming, mostly. Especially the rounder China doll with long bangs and braided pigtails who did your feet. But sometimes even she'd look up suddenly and say something wongy to the manicurist who would then throw a sour look at you. And you'd be stuck there with the wongy gossip and toxic goop.

"Pick your cull–ah. You pick your cull–ah."

Pink Corvette. Violet Femme. Eight Lays A Week. Pearly pinks, drop dead reds, and winter wine. I chose the same ballerina pink I always used, and they glued a tiny gold Mercedes charm to a fingernail on my right hand. Ezze had French tips. Devon liked hooker red. Ash went with teal and rust stripes and a hoop charm that dangled from the tip of her almost–pinky nail.

"What are we doing tonight?" Devon asked, looking over her shoulder. She was asking Ash, but Ezze answered.

"Let's drink at Ash's first and then go straight to the party so we don't have to deal with parking. We should get ready kind of early. Ron, can you stay at Ash's this weekend? My parents will lie for you."

"Um...yeah."

Somewhere then I trailed off into the chemical pong of countless mini fans and twangy gossip.

I found my grasshopper self at an electric organ store in a very brown mall, looking up at a crate of sale records. I pulled out the only one

I could reach. It had the face of evil on it with devil makeup and samurai hair, black lipstick and dripping blood. With a big red sticker for $2.99. Yes! My first real freedom! I walked through the very brown organ–slash–miscellaneous–electronics shop, placing the evil record proudly onto the counter. The vested salesman stopped what he was doing, looked at the record and then at me. I held up a five dollar bill. This was it. Me against his giant handlebar moustache and thinning hair. I want this record and, NO, my mommy is NOT with me. He rang it up and handed it back to me. I had my freedom, for 2–99, devil makeup and samurai hair. I had no idea what I had purchased, but I couldn't wait to play it backwards at Show–and–Tell. ⚡

"Ouch!" I looked at the manicurist like, "What the fuck?" She had cut the cuticle a little too close to the flesh. It stung and part of me thought she had done it on purpose. Maybe because of the glazed look I must have had on my face. Maybe because we were getting our nails done when we should have been in school. I glared at her and she smiled back at me suspiciously. She wasn't the lady who had done my mother's perfect Dynasty red nails for years. So I didn't really know her. My mother and I were opposites. I wore my hair wild and she wore hers like Jackie Collins. She despised my partying, and I guess the adventures she never had. "This is NOT A HOTEL!" she'd inform me like a dark shadow when I wobbled in at 3 a.m. She was ferocious about it, even though she was paying for my chonchy dresses and slutty stockings with the seam up the back. I mean, I had the sluttiest heels out of all my friends. Courtesy of Ms. Dynasty. It was so confusing. She knew what I was doing and dressing me for it, and then punishing me at the same time. She gave it to me with one hand and slapped me with the other. I was glad her regular nail lady was off today. But even if she was, that lady would never rat on me.

Then I overheard a familiar but annoying voice behind me. I thought it sounded like they were talking to Ash and Ezze. "What's up, guys… blah blah blah…we heard about that party."

Ezze's aloof voice followed, "Oh, you did?"

"Yeah, from those boys who always hang out with you guys. We met them last weekend at some random party we went to."

Oh GOD. It was Goldie Locks and her Twinkie Twin who rarely spoke. I didn't dare turn around. My stomach felt sick. Even though I couldn't see her, and she wasn't really talking, I could feel the fire behind Ash's eyes.

"Oh, *really*? How was it?" I could hear Ezze sort of mocking those Twinkie Twinks. She could have been a politician. She was soooo slick.

"It was rad. Those boys are total babes! Especially the one with the dimples..."

The one with the dimples? Which one was that? Fuck. It must be THE FANG! I couldn't move because I had nail goop all over my hands and hearing them say that was fucking torture. I mean, did they know I was listening?

"Uh–huh...yeah, the boys definitely get around..." Ezze said. Goddamn she was cool. She didn't ask for any more details and the Twinkie Twinks didn't offer anything more up, except for a couple of fake smiles.

"Well, maybe we'll see you there. Bye."

"Uh–huh. See ya!" I could hear Ezze blowing on her nails. I'm sure Ash felt sick to her stomach because she was thinking about Pritchard the way I was thinking about The Fang, and it sucked. After I heard them walk through the door, I shot around to Ezze. She continued to blow on her nails calmly.

"Don't worry, little one. We don't know who they were talking about. They were probably talking about Carter." Ash was also looking at me, but for once she was silent. I kept looking at Ezze, but she just kept blowing. So I gave it up and turned back around. The nail lady shot a weird crocodile smile at me. It felt like a shovel to my gut, and the cold metal sent a shiver to my mind.

After the gold Mercedes charm finally set into the acrylic, I moved to the nail dryers at the front of the salon. Ash and Devon and Ezze were already there and their nails were almost dry.

"I'm starving. And tired," I moaned. But it was way more than that.

"Let's go to the mall." Devon agreed.

Ezze looked at her Diana Ross nails and sprayed her fingers and pedicured toes with SUPREME DRY. "Fucking stoners," she muttered with a little laugh.

"I think Tina and Tess were going to the mall, too, to get something to eat," Syd added.

"What the fuck are you talking about? Tina doesn't fucking eat!" Ash let out.

Like I said before, there was a time when *everyone* puked. In junior high. I'm not sure if Tess did. She had those other tricks to stay skinny. I had tried to chum twice, but it was so much fucking work to puke shit up that instead I went on some crazy diet I got out of *The Enquirer*, that took me back to a pre–boob 95 pounds.

We parked by the mall's east entrance near Percico's Pizza, where there was always talk about roaches in the sauce and drug deals at the register. Some of the non–pro skaters and a lot of the stoner boys worked there. Matty worked there, too, until he got escorted away by two men in white coats after his parents realized he was on acid all the time. It was just like the movies. One second he was baking, and the next he was getting dragged off to some faraway rehab where no one could reach him. Leaving me stuck with Dead tickets for the New Year's Eve show in Oakland. Ezze and I planned the adventure with Matty who offered to drive us in his VW bus. Without him, there was no way up.

Despite the bugs, drugs, and busts, everyone still ate at Percico's. I ordered a cheese slice and so did Dev and Ezze. They were always nuclear yellow with thick drops of grease floating on top the way greasy cheese pizza should be. Even though Devon normally ate like a rabbit, she was known to pound on junk food especially tacos from Jack–off–in–the–Box. Ash refused. We took our slices outside. Tina and Tess had parked next to Ash's Big Red Bronco, waiting for us.

For some reason, the parking lot was nearly vacant, and it felt like we were the only life around. But I knew there were plenty of things going on behind the dense bushes that lined the mall's exterior. Suzee and I got dragged up there once when we were in 7th grade by some scary Madonna–wannabe bullies who claimed I had "made faces" at them going down the escalator. They forced us outside and behind the bushes, where two dudes with river bowl cuts sat divvying 8–balls up on an overturned cardboard TV box.

Tina stood there in her all–white outfit, which was the opposite of her all–dark self. She was wearing a cropped white tee over a long white knit skirt and white boots with fringe that slouched down. And she had really big little girl hair. She dressed well, but she could never be as pretty as any of the other girls. No matter how skinny she got. Or how much money her boney arms waved around.

"I've only eaten one bag of chips in three days," she sang. No one reacted, but Ezze did wrap her arms around Tina's waist. We couldn't believe the way Ezze was kissing her scrawny tanned ass. The rest of us stood there watching. It was so lame I lost my appetite. Ash's deadpan stare was locked on Tina. I couldn't tell if she wanted to be her. Or beat her.

I opened the back door of the Big Red Bronco and scooted onto the seat. Devon got in, too. She didn't care about Tina. Ash stood there, waiting for Ezze. Tess was so damn tolerant; I just didn't get what she saw in Tina. I took a giant red apple out of my bag and started twisting the stem.

"A…B…C…D…"

Devon looked over at me and laughed.

"Damn, Ron. I wish we had that roach."

"E…F…G…I know…"

Ash and Ezze got inside.

They yelled out the window as we drove off, "Later, Smegs!"

I sat there, wishing I had that sticky nugget. It would be hours until I was sent to the back of the party...

"...H…I…J." ⚡

SYDNEY

⚡ Despite Sydney Christmas–Yorke's nonstop partying, she always looked bright and perky for her job as a perfume model at the mall. But I never understood how she knew when to get to work because one of her favorite things to say was, "I don't know how to tell time." She was almost proud of it. Playing dumb was somehow her power and she especially used that exaggerated faux blondeness whenever there was a cute boy around. It was nauseatingly painful to listen to—*if* you knew her. Because Syd was no dummy. Except maybe when it came to boys.

There were impressions of Sydney that only we knew to be totally false. Yes, she was mousey with large brown eyes and a perfectly sprayed mane of ratted feathers in perfect sandy shades. Yes, she was in a lot of special ed. classes, even if she didn't need to be. When it came to school, she was more or less just lazy. The homework was minimal, allowing her to cruise through high school the same way she cruised through life, totally carefree. She did have some ambition, though. All along she knew she either wanted to work with makeup, or maybe become a nurse, and a mother one day. And, like a lot of girls, Syd got married every time she fell in love. You know what I mean.

She wore teal pinstripe Polo oxfords tucked into baby pink stretch leggings with high heel pumps. She had zebra print minis and hot pink everything and was always well put together, even though she definitely wasn't one of the rich girls. But even her light heart couldn't stop all the bullshit rumors around her and about her. Like, they said she was some slutty cheerleader—having been on the squad in junior high—when actually she had serious longterm boyfriends the entire time I knew her. And you'd NEVER catch Syd sucking some mutt's dick in some bathroom at some party ever. I guess if people see you're pretty and they think you're rich, too, that's enough to make them all hate you. Yeah, a lot of people who didn't know her at all thought she was loaded, because her outfits were new and fantastic and her BJ was always the perfect blonde. The truth is, she was just smarter than they thought. Syd knew *exactly* how her ditsy rep' could work for her. She *really* understood that power.

Unlike her fake friends who stuck by her because she was cute, we got to see her when she wasn't working it. When you ended up alone with her and really watched her talk, you got to see *her*. Behind the the makeup there was really so much sorrow cutting through those big brown eyes. Syd was so strong; she'd cry for a minute and straighten up and put the makeup back on.

As for her façade, Syd was a charmer who had all the girls (and boys) in her pocket. At a moment's notice, she could borrow anything from anyone's closet: white fringe boots, leather dresses, lipstick, leather jackets, dance dresses, bras, underwear, tampons, jewelry, even homework. But that didn't mean she was shallow. Syd was the one who kept in touch during the summer, mailing endless postcards and letters during faraway places. Syd was the one who kept in to call you to meet her for girl talk at the Old Moppet's Coffee and Pie Shoppe by the mall. The place reeked of old people smell, but we loved their potato–cheese soup with cornbread and a slice of coconut cream pie we'd split. It was one of her favorite things to do, and we went every week. She was the one who wasn't afraid to say she fucked up. Like when she took a "fast money" cocktailing gig in Texas for a month one summer and gave it up after a night when she did "coke–o–puffs" (shots lined with coke) and woke up the next day topless with a $700 wad stuffed in her scrunchy white sock. She called her mother that very second with an SOS message—"I want to come home!" She had no problem admitting that she was "so so wrong." ⚡

She wore her braces like they were bedazzled and giggled at everything. A lot of times she laughed so hard her mascara would run. The only true thing was that her boyfriends were never good to her and never good enough for her. They were all cocky and lame and thought they were the shit because they had this trophy girlfriend in the palm of their hand. Ezze's older brother was one of the worst. He wasn't good looking or real or ambitious or smart or anything. After they finally broke up, he went after Taylor and other girls we knew. It sickened me. Syd never really said too much about it. Until one night when we were drunk in the parking lot at Bob's Big Boy killing time until the cops left the party and we could head back. She didn't get mad. Or have a fit. She only looked at me and asked, "Why would he do that?"

Sometimes she worked in the office and wrote us re–admit slips, just like Taylor, and sent smoke signals when the Office Hags were busting students. She took modern dance class seriously in her one–shoulder teal leotard and black Caputzio dance shoes. Syd signed the back of her dance pictures with silly messages:

RONNIE, HERE IS YOUR UGLY PICTURE!
BUT YOU LOVE ME PRETTY OR UGLY!
I LOVE YOU! LET'S GET WASTED!
XOXO LIL' SYD!

Syd had perfect hair and a perfect body and perfect outfits and almost perfect teeth, I never felt less than perfect around her; not only was she a total babe, but she was also a total stroker. Even if she chatted it up with money girls at snack because they had all been cheerleaders together in junior high. Really, she could have gone that route and been one of them if she had really wanted to. But they were flavorless to her. A total bore. She'd rather spend time ratting my bronze brown hair out and running electric blue liner on my waterline.

Once, I mentioned a girl in our dance class to Syd. The girl, Melanie Loonberg, was sweet and shy and nice to me. And incredibly pretty with a tiny ballerina body, full auburn hair, and light blue doll eyes. "Why doesn't anyone talk to her?" I asked.

"I don't know, Ron," she answered. "But you talk to her. And that's nice."

The first time I went to her house, I was more than surprised. When I only knew her from afar, I never imagined she and her mom and dad lived in a tiny apartment practically under a freeway. The complex didn't even have a pool, and most apartment buildings normally did. It was lodged between the uppities and what the Hoity Toity's considered the lows. What shocked me even more was her intense honesty. She didn't make any excuses for her small apartment or her tiny bedroom. Nope. No giant waterbed. No separate entrance. No giant mirrored closet doors. She didn't have any cars. She didn't even have a garage. What she did have was her integrity. Syd was the same person, whether we were at a party, amid school bullshit, or at her home.

"This is my mom and this is my dad," she said, introducing me that first day. "This is Ronnie." Her parents were older; her dad had a stroke or something and looked stern and stuck in a wheelchair. To my surprise, however, he cracked a little smile under his right brow.

"Were you a cheerleader, too?" he asked.

"No, dad. Ronnie hates that stuff. Ron doesn't have to do that stuff. She doesn't have to do any of that stuff. She's more of an artist." I couldn't believe it. I didn't even know Syd knew about my interest in art. We never talked about that stuff. But here it was.

"Ooooh. So *you're* the artist." He seemed even more interested now. Her mother watched, from the kitchen behind him. The kitchen was more of a kitchenette almost—inside their cozy living room. Syd's dad was lodged in between.

"Yeah. I guess. Well, not really, yet." I mouthed slowly and shot Syd a nervous smile. I was a little frightened of her dad because I heard he didn't like most of our friends. I never thought for one second Syd had talked to her dad about me or my interest in art.

"It takes a lot of guts to be an artist," he said, as if to go back in time, before he was a dad, before he had kids, before he had a stroke. "And your people are supposed to be good artists, aren't they?" I just smiled.

I knew what he meant and didn't take offense.

"GOD, DAD!" Syd motioned for me to follow her into the tiny, carpeted hallway that ran to her room. "Come on, Ronnie." But when we got to her room, she giggled a little and whispered, "Damn, Ron. My dad fucking loves you! He NEVER talks to anyone!"

I never looked at her the same way after that visit. The way the entire school looked at her. People thought she was a lot like the Twinkie Twins. But those girls repulsed Sydney and she never had anything to do with their sticky ways. There was no shame. No lying. No feelings of being less than. She was proud of where she was at, where she had come from. Or unfazed by what she was supposed to be.

On Christmas, Syd gave us candy or sexy 3–for–$5 panties, depending on if she had money or not, tucked into personalized plastic drinking cups that she'd decorate in puffy Day–Glo ink, just like Tess. Every joint of every letter had a big dot like they did in cheerleading except our cups had all of our favorite sayings including the two that were hers and hers alone: "WOOOOHOOO" and "SOMF!" (SIT ON MY FACE). Sydney also dotted her I's and everything else with hearts.

I was in on most of her secrets, even though a lot of them happened on trips that I wasn't on, because I was always grounded. I was ALWAYS grounded, even once for an entire summer for staying out late. One of the skaters called me "girl in a coma" when I reappeared at a Repulsors' party when the school year started. Newt was the most famous—and radical—pro skateboarder from Sketchwood, which, for its very small landscape, had managed to produce a dozen or so stars. He was slutty and out of control, a drug addict who had flatlined and been jailed so many times that no one batted an eyelash when he wasn't around. He was a skate god who racked in ridiculous amounts of money, mostly because of his psychotic joker antics. It was all about his image. Once after a night of raging, Ezze, Syd, and I needed a ride to Rif's house. We rode with Bardy, the lead singer of The Repulsors and also one of Newt's best friends. That night Bardy pressed us to follow him to yet another party. He was skeleton skinny back then because of speed, and this was a strange time when he and

Ezze were hooking up hooking up. So Ezze sat shotgun while Syd and I fell over each other in the backseat. We were just too damn drunk.

At some point, en route to Rif's, Syd's Dooky&Pork purse capsized at her feet. Of course Syd thought it was funny as hell, but anything could be if you were that drunk in a backseat. We both leaned down and grabbed handfuls of spilled junk at her feet, stuffing whatever we could into her bag.

"What the hell are you two doing?" Ezze asked, finally taking her attention away from Bardy and her hair fluffing for a few seconds.

"Nothing," Syd giggled.

We crammed all we could into the preppy handbag until the car stopped. We were at Rif's and so totally drunk that we literally tumbled over ourselves in laughter getting out of the car. As we wobbled toward Rif's bedroom window, Ezze stayed back in the car with Bardy. Syd pushed the curtains to the open bedroom window aside and saw Rif's bitter face waiting to rip us one.

"You guys are going to wake my mom up," she groaned. Rif thought she was tough the same way Ash thought she was tough. But Rif was truly tough to the core. I mean, she was the first person I ever heard of to have a clit ring.

Syd and I were still giggling, but we managed to whisper, "Sorry… Sorry." Syd crawled in first and I followed into the extra twin–sized bed. It was where we always ended up if we were too wasted to go home. Rif acted cranky, but she wasn't really. It was part of her persona to look pissed off all the time. Syd and I stripped down to our bras and panties and got under the covers, still quietly laughing. Trying to stop was pretty hopeless.

"You guys, come on. Stop it. I'm tired," Rif growled in the darkness. But that just made us laugh harder. Even though she was starting to get really annoyed, we could sort of hear Rif give in and crack a smile. "Fuuuuuck," she moaned just as Ezze's leg, arm, and head popped through the curtain.

"Woohooo!" Ezze whistled slowly. It was her Ezze–got–some cat call. At some point, I don't remember when, we all fell asleep. The three of us in one tiny bed and Rif in her queen.

In the morning, Rif got up and left the room. Ezze and Syd sat in bed laughing. I listened as the girls gave the play–by–play recap of the night before, which is what they always did.

"What the hell were you two laughing about last night?" Ezze asked.

Syd got up, pulled the wedgy out of her perfect ass, then stopped and smiled her bracey smile. "Ooh fuck!" she said walking over to the dresser by the window. "My bag fell over and everything dumped out and we couldn't stop laughing..." But as she got closer to the Dooky&Pork, her voice faded out. She picked up the unzipped, overstuffed bag with lots of envelope ends sticking out of its top. "What the fuck?" Then she sat on Rif's bed and placed the purse on her lap. She pulled one envelope out after another, investigating their contents, then stacking them neatly beside her on the lemon yellow daisy bedspread. "Fuck, dude! These are Newt's checks!" Ezze and I leapt up, our hands reaching for the pile. There were just under a dozen checks. One for 10,000. One for 5,000. Another one for 5,000. Another for 1,500. And most were for "demos."

"Oh, fuck!" Ezze laughed. "Well, get ready because he's gonna be piiiiisssed!"

Not two minutes later, Rif walked in with a beer in one hand and the cordless phone in the other. "It's Newt—" she said, handing the phone over to Syd. "He sounds pissed!" As Syd took the phone from Rif, she looked at us, and her bracey smile widened.

Hey, Syd! What time is it?

"Hold–up wait–a–minute let–us put–some BOOM in it." ⚡

It had only been three weekends since that magical night with The Fang. And only two weekends since the dumb dance where he gutted me like I was diseased. ⚡

We had sat in his metallic green '68 Mustang with the cut–up black interior and kissed and kissed until he found a little hole on my inner thigh in the seam of my white with black polka–dot leggings. I had slowly put my hand on the fingers that gently poked inside. The Fang pulled his hand away and slowly detached his lips from mine, still smiling a little in a half–lid daze, enough for me to know everything was okay. I usually felt calm and at ease; it was so easy to just be myself with him. I didn't know how else it could be.

"Yeah," he whispered through his stony perma–grin as he moved back into driver's position. "Maybe I should calm down," he muttered to himself.

I didn't say anything. I didn't move. I just sat there smiling a little at his non–admitting admittance. This was never about a challenge or a fuck or anything like that. I knew he truly felt something real for me. He turned the keys in the ignition, putting his other hand on the wheel, and I sat back. Then he pulled me down so my head lie back on his lap, looking up at him, with the steering wheel was just above me. He leaned down and kissed me and we laughed. I tried to get up as he backed out of the parking lot, but he quickly leaned down again and kissed me.

"No! Stay there." He laughed. And I laughed. He drove onto the street, with me blinded from where we were or where we were going. But I was happy as hell to be so adored by him. About every five minutes, he'd slow down as if we'd hit a stoplight and lean in to kiss me. Then he turned the car off and kissed me harder. I lifted my head up and looked out, realizing we were parked right there in the middle of the main avenue, with no one around. I was laughing, but a bit confused, surprised, and very happy.

"You can't park in the middle of the street! Turn the car on!"

The Fang laughed.

"Okay," he said and turned the car back on, insisting I "stay down." But after a couple minutes, he stopped again, turned the engine off, and started making out with me. I peeked out and realized we were, once again, parked in the middle of the street. This went on for about 10 more blocks maybe. When we got to Helmet's house The Fang started to kiss me, but he paused right before he reached my eager lips. The silliness erased from his face and his eyes became incredibly serious as his eyes looked onto mine.

"I know you," he whispered. I couldn't move. I couldn't think. I couldn't vomit because he was above me. I only looked up at him and smiled (I think).

Only a couple weeks after that "I know you" night, the dumb dance happened, and I hadn't even had a chance to ask him about what he said to me that night in front of Helmet's house in the '68 Mustang. Not that I would have. But, maybe. Maybe I'd see him tonight. I was sure he'd be here. ⚡

It was one of the biggest Repulsor parties of the year—ten kegs, a huge stage, and permission from the entire block to party until midnight.

The night had begun—almost. It was tradition for the girls to start a big night off with a "dinner" at Humahuma Nooka's. It was our thing. I don't think anyone else from Sketchwood ever went there. But we'd meet there—Ash, Tess, Ezze, Devon, Rif, Taylor, Sydney (if we were lucky) and me. Sometimes Tina would be there. But more often than not, she was busy fucking someone's boyfriend, or planning to, snorting lines and hiding out, or puking and buying her Cuntempo's outfit for the night.

But who cared? Tonight was special. Taylor and Rif and Sydney and Tess were all here. And Sydney and Tess were here without their boyfriends. We piled out of the two cars into the Tiki–lined parking lot. ⚡

Humahuma Nooka's was a million years old and in the strangest wasteland location. Way down southeast of Sketchwood was the lost town of Dustbynn, a place that made our neck of the woods look like Bel Air. There was a duck farm, a pine tree nursery, a really old '70s "Mountain Kahuna Apartments" building, a used lowrider car sales lot and body shop, and Humahuma Nooka's, with its giant palm trees and banana–leaved shrubbery, and giant Tikis. The façade looked plastic and faded, but in a good way, like the submarine ride at Disneyland or even miniature golf à la Tucson, Arizona circa 1976.

And no matter how light or bright it was outside, inside it was always casino dark, like the belly of an old pirate ship. Dim, maze–y, with booths and tables sectioned off by freestanding "walls" of wooden pier trunks and other "lumber", plastic seaweed, and huge aquarium tanks showcasing gigantic salt water fish.

"Eight," Ash smiled at the host with her leggy lashes.

The whole place always felt incredibly cokey and wrong somehow, but in a very right way. I always felt like shit was going on in the shadowed corner booths, and the reason why we always got away with shit there was because they just wanted us drunk and distracted and gone.

Ash sat at the end of the giant table, like always, because she was so damn tall. Then everyone else flopped down and pulled out or arranged their fake driver's licenses. One by one, each of us recited (to ourselves) the trick questions we might be quizzed on to prove our IDs were legit, with eyes dead ahead, up and to the side, or else if some weren't quite sure, down on our laps and sort of under the table scanning the ID itself. Some of the girls had more than one fake ID— usually a pretty good one from an older sister that was expired and another unexpired one as a back up. And even though the unexpired backup was often a terrible match, you always brought it because you just never knew when someone might need an ID. We were always prepared. Because if one of us went down, we ALL went down. Ash and Rif had it the hardest. They were lucky they each had their older sister's valid license. I mean, come on...Ash was too tall and Rif was too extreme to use just any fake ID.

We all took a moment of silence, going over our fake birthdates, fake birth places, fake addresses, fake zodiac signs, fake excuses why the ID's were expired or why they were out of state, as well as memorizing the fake spellings of the fake addresses, fake names, and anything else fake we thought they might catch us on. We had done Humahuma Nooka's a couple of times a month for almost a year, but we still couldn't recognize the staff. Somehow, though, I felt they recognized us. Whatever. They were all probably snorting coke and smoking bowls in the back of the fish tanks anyway. ⚡

The waiter who was young and Greek or something approached us and stood at the corner of our table between Ash and Devon's seats. Our bodies tensed up and we all connected eyes with a somewhat toothy, dead smile. Ready? FUCK YEAH! The reason why Humahuma Nooka's was so dear to us was the sheer fact that we could drink A LOT for not a lot of money. Not to mention, we could be in a restaurant and drink. "Nooki–Nooki Bowls" went along with the theme of the place, and a long way. There were a variety of ingredients and liquors, but the idea was always the same—a lit candle thing in the middle of a huge wooden salad bowl filled with rum or vodka or tequila and juice, and three or four long straws.

The light was almost green. But first we had to order food. We thought that might deter them from busting us, even though it was so totally obvious what we were here to do. Everyone tried acting dainty and refined, like we were 27 or at a fucking tea party or something. When none of us had EVER been to a tea party.

There were a lot of us, which translated into a huge tip, and we knew the waiter would take this very important detail into account when he was checking our IDs. We weren't dummies.

"Are you ready to order?"

Ash looked up and her eyes sort of popped open then.

"Yeah, we're ready," she said in her sweeter–than–sin voice. ⚡

Ash sat in black cropped T–shirt with studs and rhinestones and big blonde bangs, micro–mini black leather skirt and black fringed boots that scrunched down: "I'll have a baked potato." Toothy.

Devon in black Danzig T–shirt with upside down horned skull, black leather pants, and black boots: "I'll have a side salad with blue cheese." No smile.

Rif in cut up Repulsors' T–shirt that showed a lot of her big boobs, black longer leather skirt, and black slouchy boots covered in studs, bleached–out hair with black roots, pasty foundation (and lips), and thick thick black eyeliner: "I don't know what I want yet. Can you come back to me?"

"Sure."

Me in tight black scoopneck shirt with 3/4–sleeves above black leggings, oversized leather biker jacket and my favorite party heels with the metal tips on the toes. "I'll have a baked potato."

Sydney in turquoise spandex off–shoulder long sleeve dress that hiked up below her ass, giant blonde feathered hair and huge hoop earrings, hot pink lipgloss and snakeskin pumps: "I'll have a baked potato and a side salad with ranch and can you bring extra ranch for the potato, too, please?"

"Sure."

Tessa in black spaghetti–strap tank and black denim cropped jacket, leopard print leggings and black scrunched down suede boots with fringe and lots of gold chains and charms: "I'll have a regular salad with ranch, please. Thank you."

Taylor in cut-off white tank top, cropped white denim jacket and micro–mini, white scrunched down socks and white Reeboks: "I'll have a baked potato and a side salad with blue cheese, too, please. Thanks."

Ezze in her loose white see–through linen tank with no bra and black denim skirt, dragon lady nails, and python stilettos: "I'll have a baked potato and a side salad and can you put the butter on the side and can I also get some ranch for my potato, please?"

"Sure."

Then the waiter went back to Rif who had put her menu down and was patiently waiting like a grown up for him to come back to her. She was the only one who ordered real food. We always figured the real food from Humahuma Nooka's was gross, but she was fearless about *everything* really which helped us look totally legit. And I know some of us were secretly relieved that one of us ordered an entire meal.

"I'm hungry. I'll have that special steak thing—the Captain Combo—with a baked potato and blue cheese on the side," she said in her deeper raspy voice. "And make the steak really rare. Like RAW." Rif really did like her meat.

While the waiter rigorously wrote the order down as if he hadn't anticipated a full order from the last freak of the bunch, Ash went for it.

"We also wanted to order some drinks." He looked up and the clench under the table got harder.

"Okay," And then it came, "Can I see your ID's?"

We all moved our hands from our laps to the top of the table, handing him the ID's, one by one. He pretended to look, nod, and moved onto the next girl. It was bullshit, and we loved him for it.

"Okay," he said a very exaggerated way so everyone in the restaurant would know the ID's were checked. "What can I get you?"

That was it. ⚡Our shoulders relaxed and we exhaled. Then the level of chatter began to rise.

"What do we want? Uh, two Nooki–Nooki Bowls and one Waikiki bowl…to start."

"And a Huma–Huma–Rum Bowl…"

"I wanna do shots," Devon smiled at me. "Wanna do a shot, Ronnie?"

I looked at the list. "Sticky Shark Tooth?"

"Fuck that! Tequila!" She looked at Ezze. Ash, of course, wanted a piece. "Okay, who wants shots?" Everyone answered in sync, ME! "Okay, we'll start with that tequila Cobra's Strike shot—wait maybe we should get Sex On The Beaches? Especially for the virgin over there!" smiling in my direction. Sometimes Ash could be so dense. I mean, that made me a 27-year-old virgin.

"Yeah, let's get Sex On the Beaches," Taylor said. She might have been smiling her sweet innocent smile, but she was no weak link. The girl knew how to party and that's why she was the queen.

"Okay," Ash smiled at the waiter. She already seemed kind of drunk, but she wasn't. Her words had started to slur the moment we knew we could drink. "We're going to start with eight Sex On the Beaches, and you can bring the bowls out, too."

The waiter was stoked. Because after those shots and the bowls, we ordered more shots and bowls. HumaHuma Bowls and Sticky Shark Teeth and "to–kill–ya" Sunset shots. Thank God I had a baked potato with ranch dressing in my stomach.

We fumbled out of Humahuma Nooka's after leaving a hefty thank you tip for the waiter so he'd remember us next time. Even though we wouldn't remember him.

We wobbled out past the giant Tikis that smiled something predatory our way and mumbled, "Come back...Come back...."

We piled into our cars and headed to the party, which was only about 10 minutes away. We pulled out of the parking, past the chubby palms and bamboo stalks lining the dirty old black asphalt. We were blind to everything except the black glitter sparkles inside the Big Red Bronco. ⚡

We drove through South Sketchwood, which was supposedly sub par to the rest of Sketchwood's snobbiness, but it wasn't anything near a ghetto. All the motorhead families seemed to live in South Sketchwood, including Ash's family, but she was more central which was fancier than the eastern and western lowers of our small town.

South Sketchwood had massive backyards, some with gardens and chickens, and massive multi–multi–car garages lined with massive freezers filled with massive stocks of frozen steaks and ice cream sandwiches, Steakums, pizza, Lean Cuisine, and chicken–fried steak, and of course loads of beer. So massive were the lots that the parents never really noticed if we tapped into their stash. South Sketchwood also had massive parties in those massive backyards and massive multi–car garages with those massive supplies of cold beer.

We were ridiculously drunk—and happy—and we hadn't even started. Once we did, though, we didn't *ever* stop.

"The flier said it's going to be a ten–kegger." That meant more people would be there which meant dreaded longer lines at the kegs. The beer would get sucked up faster, until the cops broke it up.

"Welllll, fuck!" Ash put her right dragon–nailed fingers laced with thin gold rings onto the volume knob of her Alpine HiFi. "We better fucking get there and get some beer, bitches!" Then she turned the music up so loud the interior walls of the Big Red Bronco started to vibrate. There were speakers everywhere—under the seats, behind the seats, in the ceiling, in the doors, in the dash, in the glove box. Our arms went up and our heads started banging, except for Ash's. She was just happy to watch it all. ⚡

We drove past oversized Monopoly houses with perfect hedges and huge old trees, brand new Benz's and old Ford pickups and Toyota MR2's, white Honda Civics, black VW Cabriolets, and copper MG Midgets, heirloom rose bushes and preppy brick houses and sterile yellow–and–green Hoity Toity houses, and all were lit by fancy porch lanterns. And almost every other lawn had a little man pointing us in the right direction. Lawn jockeys. I never understood why anyone would want a lawn jockey, a little statue of a clown–color uniformed horse rider, standing in front of their house. These were the same people who bristled and winced when they drove through neighborhoods in the cities bordering Sketchwood. Neighborhoods they deemed to be beneath their Hoity Toity standards, especially if they saw a couch on a porch—ESPECIALLY if they saw a couch on the porch. That was so ghe–tto. That was trailer park action. It made more sense to me to have an old comfy couch in front of your home than a fucking lawn jockey. It was the lameness that was old Sketchwood money. But tonight, under the heavy influence of Nooki–Nooki Bowls and Metallica, the lawn jockeys cheered us on:

This way to the keg, girls!
Get Wasted! Get Fucked Up!
Get Stoned! Then come back
and suck my little lawn jockey dick!
I'll be here waiting for you!

We would not have sucked his little lawn jockey dick. We would have snickered at their little lawn jockey dicks.

We got lost in time until the car screeched and we all jerked forward at the same time and laughed. Ash had seen the spot right in front of the house and slid right into it so we wouldn't have to trek 10 blocks to the party.

Everyone ratted their hair, put their lipgloss on, and jumped out of the Big Red Bronco. We needed more booze or beer, we needed to get cups before they were gone, and we needed to plant ourselves by the keg before the dumbass dumbasses showed up.

Somewhere along the line, Repulsors' parties got really popular. Like every high school in a 100–mile radius would show up. It was rad and sucked at the same time. We still ruled the show, though, along with the older girls like Peachy Keene. She was an international bikini model and Hollywood starfucker whose boobs were perfect and perky without ever wearing a bra and who happened to be as sweet to us as Taylor, despite how hot or famous she was. She had been shunned a slut, she had told me once—probably by less attractive wealthy bitches with terrible Sheena Easton frosted hair and thick thick necks and braces and squinty eyes—because she was naturally hot and naturally cool and everyone wanted to fuck her, obviously. Peachy didn't come from money, so the dumbasses and the DeeDee's had labeled her a whore—without any evidence—just to ruin her life. It didn't work, though, because Peachy was as real as real could be.

"But you weren't a slut, right?" I had candidly asked her one night, looking up at the 5–foot–10 bleached high–ponytailed girl with perfect cheekbones.

"No. But they started calling me a slut before I even started high school. So I was like, 'If they're going to call me a slut, then I'll be a slut,'" she said proudly. It was like she could see the game way before the rest of us and she knew, in the end, she'd still be hot 20 years later and have great stories to laugh about and all those fuckers would end up PTA moms with fat asses and wrinkles all over their too–many–tans leathered and weathered faces. She admittedly slept with all of their boyfriends just because she could. Peachy fucking ruled. ⚡

At the Repulsors' party, those lameass Crystal Lite bitches stood clear of her. And clear of us. We knew who we were and this was our territory.

The weather was warming up, but the breeziness left over from the winter air still lingered around. The night was cool and warm at the same time, locked into medium blue twilight. Perfection. There a thousand cars sardined in a cul de sac below Longdong Drive. and we could see the backyard full of bright light and party noise.

My stomach was in knots even though I was laughing and smiling. No amount of alcohol would or could erase the feelings hiding behind my stiff brow. Was he here? Why hadn't I heard from him? Was that it? In my heart he had always been mine. But now I fidgeted with the ratted dry ends of my wavy hair. I wondered if I was pretty enough, thin enough, cool enough, sexy enough, anything enough, everything enough. Even in the perfectness of tonight and I couldn't get it out of my head. I was totally mindfucked. Really, no one ever heard me whine or cry when I got drunk or high. I was only doing what felt natural. But really it was anything but natural. I was lipglossing and spraying and chanting let's–get–drunk calls and just happy, or playing happy, to be in a place where I'd be wrapped in a blanket of acceptance and no one would point out what was going on inside my head. That severe crackling somewhere behind the glass of my eyes. The girls were too drunk to worry and everyone had their own agendas anyway. And *anything* could happen. You just never knew what adventures you'd be rehashing the next day.

But for a minute, I felt less than. Mentally, I was looking back at my dented self, using the tips of my filed acrylic nails to dig into my skin, raking them from the top of my forehead over my thick–but–groomed brow, through my eyelids, over the thin skin of my eyes, in and over my blushed cheeks, under my chin where the foundation line sometimes showed if I didn't blend it in, over my décolleté and fleshy C–cups, into the grooves of my ribs, ripping down the sides of my little beer belly and hips and deep into my hated thighs, through my scarred knees, down the side of my calves until I ended at the corners of my Achilles heels. And just as I felt the warm gush, I started at the top again—slowly slowly slowly raking down down down. All the while, chit–chatting hello and hosing beer down my throat. Lost in the mutter of drunken chaos and bright diagonal lights of the backyard. All of a sudden I realized I had no idea where the girls had gone.

What had I done? Here I was again, with everyone and no one. ⚡

Crowded Repulsor parties were like a Cracker Jack pool—pushing through the clusterfucks and nonsense banter, I never knew if just behind the slobbery scammers or the circle jerks, he'd jump out and surprise me. It sucked. I kept drinking and felt foggier and everything got louder.

I remember telling someone I was going to be sick and running into the house. I don't remember too much except that I leaned over and chummed hard into the bathtub when I was sitting on the toilet. I might have been passed out for an hour. Or five. I might have only been in there for 10 minutes. It was more like I had puked and passed out with my leggings and cherry print panties down at my steel–tipped stilettos, and my right cheek glued to the cool bathtub rim, with a bit of vomit dried in the corner of my mouth and drip dried between that corner and my shin.

I woke up, ratted my hair, Listerined four times, and went back into the yard for round two. The party was in full force. After getting a new beer and smoking out on the way around—"Ronnie! Want a hit?"—"Ronnie, wanna get high?"—"Ronnie! Come here a sec!"—I was fucked up again, especially because my stomach was empty.

After walking halfway around the backyard, I saw The Fang's friends. Helmet was silent and grunting under his mound, Pritchard was goofy and eyebrowed and wasn't tough, but he was pure Metal, and Ash was hovering over him with wild eyes and drool at her lips. Carter was acting his dumb–dumb I'm–too–sexy self. He was the hottest to me when I had first met him, but now his rockstar features had morphed into an ogre and there was no going back once I saw him that way. Ezze was near Helmet fiddling with her hair, always playing like she'd get him one day. He never gave her more, though, than a short grunt. Then again, that was more than he gave a lot of people.

Dusty Smalls was on his way over to me with his cheery smile. He was one of two male rockers who were Asian and total Heshers and totally amazing. The other was Eugene, a super Speed Metal dude with razor cut shiny long hair and friends with one of the Tommy's. He was in the Repulsors and a lot like Dusty. Except Dusty was older Metal with shorter hair, AC/DC, Sabbath, And I was closer to Dusty. He gave me sweet attention and was one of The Fang's best friends, I always was like, well, fuck, of course The Fang loves me. But tonight Dusty wasn't as hyper in his fitted Levi's jacket and jeans.

"Hey, Ron–nee……what's up?" He greeted me the "normal" way, but written all over his face were feelings of confusion and guilt and just the plain old truth that he and the boys thought The Fang was letting "it" all waste away on someone unimpressive. Well, that's what it felt like anyway. One by one the boys sweetly joked around, but really they were overcompensating like they had wronged me. All it did was slice me in two and whatever faith I had poured right out into the Budweiser–soaked grass under my feet.

"Nothing much. Let's get high…" was all I could say. ⚡ I felt my middles melt into vomit. I definitely knew something was up now. And I'd know soon. Tomorrow at the Roxy show. I didn't want to know. But I really didn't have a choice.

I genuinely liked the boys and the way they always respected me. Even when Pritchard was rolling his eyes over Ash's shoulder at me, as she dug her eager tongue down his throat, like I was on his team. (She was taller than Pritchard so she had to bend her knees a little to really get in there.) Pritchard freed himself from Ash's claw and started cracking jokes. "What's up, trouble?" he said, blowing a smoke cloud above my head. I smiled, said nothing, and looked up. "Are you having a good time, Ronnie, Ronnie? What the fuck, dude? Ronnie Ronnie? You're having fun, right, Ron?" The more they fussed, the more I knew. They might as well have been using megaphones:

WE FEEL LIKE SHIT!
WE LIKE YOU!
WE KNOW OUR FRIEND IS HURTING YOU

AND TO TOP IT OFF
WE FEEL EVEN WORSE
BECAUSE THAT CHICK SUCKS!!!
WE DON'T KNOW WHAT TO DO
'CAUSE WE ACTUALLY CARE ABOUT YOU!
WE KNOW HE'S BEING AN IDIOT!

I just felt more drunk, more high, more dizzy. More lost. Why did I care—if he wasn't even *there*? He was the only one NOT here, because he was with that other girl. A SO–LAME girl. The lights above the trees and the clear night sky and the ground kept getting closer and people were starting to scurry because someone said, "The cops are coming!" and I was getting bumped out of the way and pushed here and grabbed there and little voices whooshed past my ears in diagonal directions…

Ronnie…The cops are coming…Ronnie…Who'd you come with?… Ronnie…I think Ash left…Ronnie…Was he here?…Ronnie… After–party at Tommy's!…Ronnie…Are you going to be sick?

Even though I was deep on my way to cuckoo town, vomitous grass and hair and clothing and probably right in front of a cop where I'd surely be arrested and my throat slit and I'd be shipped in disgrace like a dead chicken to a faraway country, I managed to see Smiley coming my way. If he was horny and you had puked or were about to puke, he'd take his chances and stick his jock tongue right down your throat. He was *that* kind of guy. He was one of my first real boyfriends. But as much as he *loved* me and loved *trying* to fuck me, he was too caught up in the bullshit of show. And the more *me* I got, the more I didn't mesh with the conformity of his WASP–y cut–out world.

"Hey," he smiled. I can't remember if I answered, but when he leaned down to kiss me, things went murky. All I know is I was pissed. Pissed at *him* for not being *here* and being *there*. For pursuing me and then getting luke warm. He comes around. I like him…as a friend. I would have been perfectly fine that way even if I was still jealous at all the girls he dated. But he went for it and kept pressing it and milking it until I felt like why else would anyone share with me what he shared with me? Calm smiles and late night whispers and laughter? What else could all of that be? Apparently nothing. He was just void and gone.

⚡ I woke up in someone's bed—kid's car bed—curled in a ball, with the spins for nearly an hour. Every time I peeked, the floor would speed up frog-eyed to the ceiling just before I shut my eyes to save myself again. I finally woke up later in a seafoam of almost-vomit trickling out from the left corner of my mouth that trailed into a dry line down the side of the bed into a fried-egg puddle on the floor. Yep. I scratched my left eyebrow with my right hand. I could feel the clumps of mascara sticking my eyelashes together. I stumbled out of the room in last night's now-hobo clothes to find someone I knew. I didn't know whose preppy house I was in, and I was still a little drunk.

I walked into the pine tree family room with comfy plaid sofa-lined walls of light beechwood panels that framed a huge TV. I realized we were at Tommy's. There was everyone, passed out over each other, wall-to-wall couched bodies. Clothed, but so out they were close to dead. No one budged as I stood there—not knowing what to do.

I cut a piece of Entenmann's coffee cake, poured a tall glass of water. I sat down at the comfy wood dining table that looked into the room with the couch bodies. There was a big blue bong on the table, still packed. I decided I should hit it, hoping it would make me feel less sick. And, what the hell? I knocked something off the table as I picked up the lighter, which was sitting on a mirror. I leaned down and picked up a straw that looked like McDonald's, but had been cut short. I set it on the mirror. I looked up and out into the couched bodies room at all the couch bodies. I looked back at the clean red-and-yellow striped straw. I looked down at the clean mirror. I took the lighter, and as I looked back at the couch bodies—which still hadn't moved—I took a hit. Then the phone rang, and a voice from one of the lifeless couch bodies moaned, "Ge-e-e-et thaaaaat…"

I passed out again with the couch bodies after many solo tokes and cleaning the dried vomit.

"Ronnie," Ezze softly called from the edge of the racecar bed. It was late, probably around 3 or 4 p.m. "Tess is picking us up soon. Are you hungry 'cause Tess wants to go get frozen yogurt?"

I was foggy and tired and hungry and dirty and sleepy. But the sound of Ezze's voice made it all feel fine. ⚡

"Okay," I answered, with the last bit of energy lodged in my throat. "I puked in my sleep…again." Ezze slowly shook her head. "Did you know I was sitting out there at the table for an hour while you guys were passed out?" I sat up and tried to fix the rat's nest on my head, eyeballing the floor for my shoes and purse.

"I knew you were smoking, little one," she smiled. "Get up… I'm starving."

"I saw the straw and mirror," I said quietly with my eyes fixed on her face. She probably knew it was coming, because she was already looking away into the nothingness of the room and poofing the side feathers of her hair before I even started talking. Then she stood up and walked toward the door.

"We're getting frozen yogurt or something and then panty shopping for tonight. Tess'll be here soon, so wake up and get your shit together." Then she walked out.

Get my shit together. Get my shit together? Get *my* shit together?

It was a nasty bite. Then again, she could be a morning grump, even though it was now late in the afternoon. Somehow I knew when I walked back into the room with the couch bodies, the mirror and the straw—and everything else I *hadn't* seen—would be gone. And not one person would ever bring any of it up to me or in front of me ever again. As if it had just been a dream.

Tess was always our savior. No matter how airheadish her comments were or snorty her laugh was or trendy her outfits were, they never damaged her genuine quality. She knew Ash had abandoned us (again) after too much beer, not enough attention from Pritchard, and the thought of the cops busting her Big Red Bronco. She hadn't bothered to look for us, said fuck it and left. Tess's never used her hand–medown T–Top red Camaro the way Ash did with the Big Red Bronco. And she never left us stranded, ever.

We saw the Camaro pull up and park, and out walked Tess, carrying a paint–splattered Cuntempo's bag. Ezze and I met her at the back door stairs outside the kitchen, where Ezze was smoking her Marlboro Light 100s in a box and the sun was bothering my tired eyes.

"I brought you some clothes," she said, handing the bag over to us. Her hair had been overly brushed and was light and flyaway, her blue eyeliner perfectly smudged and fresh, her lipgloss shined like pink pearl dust. She had on teal leggings and two layered tank tops, a cropped white denim jacket, and white leather slouchy boots with studs and fringe dangling from the top.

Ezze took the bag, smiled, and as she peeked inside joked, "Is this so we don't look like total hookers at the mall?" Tess smiled and looked at me, still wearing my black hooker heels in the bright daylight.

"Did you see The Fang at all? Did he show up?" She asked me.

I shook my head.

"No, but he'll be at the show tonight." Ezze's said with a smile that was grassy and light. She handed the bag over to me and smashed her cigarette out in the flowerbed. I just looked at her and tried not to puke. "Don't worry your pretty little head. Let's change and get you some hot panties for your big night!"

"Yeah, but get changed quick 'cause I'm starving," Tess pressed. I peeked into the bag and pulled out some hot pink Guess denim cut–offs. Looking at the front and then the back in sort of disbelief. "I brought those for you. I thought your butt would look cute in them. And the jelly shoes at the bottom are for you, too. They're too small for me. If they fit, you can keep them."

I just looked up at her with a confused sort of drunk really tired stare.

I never wore hot pink. Let alone, cut–off jeans. Somehow Tess always secretly styled me out—delicately peeling as many safety layers away from my shy outer self she'd get away with. Tenderly nudging me in her hyper–pink direction.

Ezze howled with a big toothy grin. "Maybe you should just wear those tonight." She was joking, of course. I'd never wear hot pink shorts to a show in Hollywood. That wasn't….well….me.

After Ezze put on a T–shirt and a narrow long black knit skirt, and I put on an oversized white T-shirt with Tess's hot pink cut–offs and black jelly shoes, we got into the T–Top Camaro. But I definitely I felt like someone else in her clothes.

Ezze sat shotgun. I sat in the backseat, wiping last night's crusty mascara from my puffy eyes. Ezze turned the stereo volume up as we pulled out of the driveway. It was one of her favorite songs. Then she started to sing in a slightly high, slightly off soft whisper, in between bits of jabber and gossip she and Tess discreetly passed back and forth. Maybe Ezze was telling her how I found the mirror and straw or maybe Tess was saying she knew something about The Fang. Or maybe they were talking about who they fucked last night. I was way too tired to crack their code.

Doo doo doo doo…Doo doodoo doo…

Blah blah…blah blah blah blah…

Blahblah….blahblah…blahblah…blah blah-blaaah…

Doo doo doo doo–oo–oo…doo doo doo doo…

Doo doo…doo doo-doo dooooo…

Blahblah….blahblah…blahblah…blah blah-blaaah…

Tess turned the volume louder.

Doo doo-doo doo doo-doo…

Oooooh…doo-doo doo-doo dooo-ooo…

Doo doo-doo doo doo-doo…

Oooooh doo doo doo doo doo…

Doo doo-doo doo doo-dooooo…

It didn't matter what was going on in the front of the Camaro. I was in my own tangled–stomach world. I was nervous about seeing The Fang tonight. My parents were going to kill me. And I was wearing hot pink cutoffs to the mall. I wanted to believe in things. But I didn't know where to start. I had believed in the wrong things my entire life, by default, with no questions answered. But like everything I was expected to be perfect, like a fucking robot. Perfect grades, perfect outfits, perfect smiles, perfect jokes, perfect face. Perfect bullshit.

"They're having an awesome sale on panties today!" Tess informed us. "They're holding the cute ones for me." She grinned a tiny–toothed grin and held it like that for a minute or two. We pulled into the Fashion Island parking lot, which was huge and pretty empty, except for the peacocks that sometimes escaped from a botanical garden nearby where they used to film Fantasy Island.

We walked straight into the mall mugginess, waving at the boys as we passed Percico's Pizza. We passed Judy's and the funny little random shop where we used to buy broken–heart friendship charms in junior high. Tess's eyes began to bulge as we approached the Day–Glo pink and orange paint–splashed shop that was Cuntempo's. I felt like puking, so I took some huge breaths and everything was racing inside my veins. But I don't think anyone noticed. Maybe they did notice and let it go, thinking it was just me. Some people got me in a second, while others who knew me since I was born never did and never will.

⚡ Maybe Tess was distracted as we walked into trendy town.

"Should we get beer for the afterparty? 'Cause we're fucked if there isn't a keg," Ezze suggested. She knew how to poise her questions in ways that convinced you without you ever knowing what she really wanted from you.

"Yeah," Tess grinned, chomping her bright pink Day–Glo gum and clawing her pink nails into the bin of thongs and g–strings. "It'll be too hard later. Will Ash go or should we go get it? That lady at Star Liquor freaked me out last time I was there."

Black lace, red lace, white lace, teal lace, turquoise lace, purple lace, hot pink lace, polka–dot lace, floral lace g–strings. Hearts and shamrocks. Cream and pink rickrack trim.

"Why was she wigging you out? I love that weird lady." Ezze looked up from the piles of panties at Tess.

Little pink bows, little white bows, little black bows, white rosettes, red rosettes, pink rosettes, black rosettes, black ribbon, and black mesh string bikinis.

"I don't know. She kept saying, 'Let ball come to you' with her Chinese accent. It was gnarly! I can't imagine being in there on coke and trying to score beer and dealing with that. I thought she was going to have a seizure or something. And her big weird boobs. She doesn't ever wear a bra, dude."

Puppies and kitties and Frenchies and dots and lightning bolts and stripes and lips and X's and O's. Rainbows and unicorns and cherries and cupids and KISS faces. I scowled at the piles of cotton and nylon and mesh and lace. I didn't know what was wrong with me.

Ezze laughed. "Crazy bitch."

"Yeah," I added. "What the fuck is that supposed to mean?"

Tess shook her head and said, "I don't know. If we go there, I'm staying in the car."

Ezze smiled. "She still sells us beer almost ever time. And they have Ronnie's 40–ouncers there for two bucks." A "Bon Chachee" song started to blast from the speakers inside trendy town.

"Oh, God. *PLEEEASE*," I whined.

"I like this song," Tess said, still digging through the piles.

"They suck. *This* sucks. Let's go…" I had to get out get out GET OUT. Though, I did buy eight pairs of black lace things and g–strings before I started to bitch. I never liked that Cuntempo's. I never understood why anyone did. It was so poseury and annoying. All the fakeness of everything everywhere, caught in one sticky spot. Packaged personality, available in a bunch of "IN" colors, so unique and original that EVERYONE at Sketchwood High was flaunting it. Maybe *that* was it. Maybe they *wanted* that "You're not the only one, bitch!" vibe? How could that be a good thing? How could my truest friends, Tess and Ezze, buy into this crap so easily? Hot pink Day–Glo Disco Stick shit. New wave plastic, and Bon Chachee blasting over it. I don't know. Maybe I was spiteful because I was never really allowed to be part of this club. I never afford those trendy pretty-girl clothes or had those cool book covers in junior high. That's how I felt about it anyway. But I had to admit that they did have really cute panties.

"What's going on over there?" Ezze looked at me.

"What?" I replied.

"Those big gruff sighs...what the fuck?"

"I didn't know I was doing that." And I meant it.

Ezze rummaged through the panties again. "I know you're not anxious to get out of here or anything," she said with a wink.

"Me? No."

"Are you worried about your parents? You're not going home until tomorrow, right?"

"Only if I have to go home."

"What'd you tell your parents?" Tess asked from behind a small mountain of plastic candy–colored lace and elastic that was nearly boob high.

"Nothing."

Tess and Ezze caught eyes for a split second. I knew what they were thinking because they had gone through this so many times with me before.

Then Ezze held up the skimpiest black lace g–string. "Here, babe," she said to me with a sneaky smile, "Why don't you get these. Maybe you'll get lucky."

"I have a pair I usually wear, just in case," I said softly

Tess quickly looked up at me. "Just in case *of what*?"

"You know…" I said.

"*You* have a pair of lucky panties?" Ezze asked, astoundment dancing on her lips.

"Uh–huh. Just one pair I like to wear when I know I'm going to see The Fang. They're my favorite. They're light blue lace Dior's. My mom got them for me." Tess and Ezze looked at each other, then back at me.

"We didn't know you were even *trying* to get lucky. Have you and The Fang even gotten close?" Ezze said.

"Not really," I said again. My face was burning. "He always stops."

Tess smiled and Ezze handed me the skimpy g–string again. "Well, maybe you should get these anyway. *Just in case* those Dior's aren't getting you there." I didn't say anything, but I did grab the g–string.

Tess wrapped her arms around the pile of candied *choñes* as if they were a small child and handed it over to the overly–trendy salesgirl who was now salivating over Tess. Her hair was frosted and short and spiky, and she was wearing a one–shoulder white sweatshirt mini dress with grommets and ribbon with a hot pink diagonal belt, a polka–dotted headband and bile–green jellies on her feet. "Are you ready?" she said with a trendy fake smile.

Silent huff. I missed him, though I'd never admit it. And Tess and Ezze just left me alone in my bubble as I walked behind them.

"What are you wearing tonight?" Tess said.

"I don't know. Can I borrow something?" Ezze answered.

"Yeah, we can go to my mom's after yogurt. I'm not sure if I'm going to the show yet. I might meet you guys at the studio afterparty."

"You should come to the show. We're all going," Ezze tried to like always to convince Tess, but that rarely happened.

"I know, but they always play the same set, and I have some homework to do. But I'll make jungle juice for you guys, even if I don't go to the show tonight." Then they carried on into more gossip and lots of stuff I didn't know about.

"…Who was Helmet with? What about him? Was he with Tina last weekend?"

"…Okay, I've fucked him and him and him and him and him and him. And, yep, him…twice…" Tess listed without a speck of regret. Without a hint of apology. I quickly woke up. ⚡

I felt stunned and bug eyed. They had all pretty much been fucked by all the mutts I despised. That repulsed me. I suspected it had all happened when we were barely out of junior high and new to high school. When the senior guys sized up the freshmen girls on the first day of school. They'd stand on each side of the main floor and rate you as you walked by. It sucked. But I got over it. I mean, I got why the boys were so happy to be seniors. Even the boys who never got any would finally get a chance. Most freshmen girls will do anything for a senior. And the boys, well…

Fresh–men. Fresh–meat.

I still felt like puking. Now even more.

We got into the Camaro, Ezze was shotgun, me in back. Still… Still… Still…Still…

Tess turned the ignition, cranked the volume—"Let's get yogurt"— and pulled out. ⚡

Doo doo doo doo...

Doo doo doo-doo-doo...

Doo doo doo-oo-oo...

Doo doo doo-doo doo doo...

Doo doo doo-oo, doo-oo, doo-oo...doo-doo-dooooo...

La la la la la la...la la la la la....

⚡

AQUA
NET
AND
SEBASTIAN NO. 9

I swear to God I might puke.

"Ronnie?! What the fuck? Dude, what the fuck is wrong with Ronnie?"

Ash's little brown and white Chihuahua, Cupcake, was overly excited with so much going on in her master's bedroom. The sun sat sandwiched between day and night. And the waterbed sat sandwiched between an oversized white dresser and an overfilled dreamy wall–to–wall closet with towering mirror doors. Our backpacks and overnight bags sat all around the pristine white carpet and on top of the bed. And her hyper little dog leapt from one bag to the next. Even with a hyperactive dog, a truck of bags, and hair flying around, everything at Ash's was always immaculate. Everything *had to be* immaculate. I noticed her modeling portfolio on top of her waterbed suspiciously opened to recent test shots. She was obviously proud of them. Especially the one of her in a pool flipping her hair back, her wet tresses caught mid–air like a huge fan. It was kind of cool.

But I needed a dooby. ⚡

It was always tricky maneuvering around the cramped room, especially with a 5–pound dog running around between your legs. We plugged a row of curling irons in: one with push–button steam, one that was skinny and long, and another metallic massive dildo–looking one. Chrome and teal, chrome and pink, and chrome and black.

Practically every free inch of space was covered with shopping bags with new lacy panties and gift–with–purchase makeup bags in every shade of blue and black eyeliner and purple, too, in matte and frosty glitter, every shade of pink lipgloss, and multiple pots of the same face powder in different transparent hues. We mixed and matched them, depending on how much we had tanned. Eyelash curlers, eyebrow brushes, tweezers. And mascara. Loads of Mascara. Mascara Mascara Mascara Mascara.

High heel boots with fringe, stiletto pumps in bubblegum and cherry, pearl white and shiny patent leather. Spandex tights, fishnets and sheer black stockings with seams up the back. Black lace garter belts and white lace garter belts, thongs and Brazilians in black lace, purple lace, with rhinestones and little bows that sit above your ass crack. Pushup bras and strapless bras and sheer silk six–string bikini tops.

Ash stood in front of the mirrored closet doors, looking over her shoulder at her white thong panty ass. Everyone had some insecurities during school hours. But when we hit Hollywood, the most skin tight scandalous pieces would come out and coat our silhouettes. Lycra, leather, cut down to there and up to there, no matter how many fatty cheese dogs we'd scarfed down that week.

"Yeah," Ash's face looked relieved as she stood there, 10–feet tall, with her nearly flat ass. "I think my new leather mini skirt is going to fit! Fuck! I starved myself all fucking week!" It was true, she did. She fidgeted through the shit dumped all over her bed, and Ezze plugged the blow dryers in.

"It'll fit," Ezze said with a wash of envy, maybe. Maybe over the new skirt, maybe over Ash's small ass. Maybe over Ash's boobs. But probably not. Ezze's lemon boobs were perfect—not too small and not too large.

Ash, still standing topless in a thong, pulled the tiny leather mini skirt over her knees and yanked and yanked it over her square–ish hips.

"Okay," she smiled, a little hunched over and out of breath. "I paid a fucking grip for this skirt, and I have to look hot tonight! I'm gonna wait a second for it to stretch before I pull up the zipper."

"You'll look hot," I said, but I didn't think anyone heard me.

"You always look good, Ash," Ezze gushed.

Syd was in her Tee and pink lace panties organizing her makeup. She had black and brown eye makeup on one eye and blue and cream on the other. "Which one looks better?" she asked Ezze.

Ash sucked in her breath, shut her eyes and with her dragon nails, pulled up the zipper with a big, "Oooooff!"

I sat there. Motionless. I always did at this point. I definitely felt like the kid of the group. I kind of liked to watch, though. Like watching your sisters.

Ash shared a canyon–dimpled smile and said, "God, I need to get laid!"

"Slut!" Syd moused out.

"Who has to take a shower after me?" Ash asked.

"Me."

"I do."

"Me, too!"

"Fuck. Someone has to shower together. Otherwise, it's going to take too fucking long. Why didn't you guys shower already?" Ash just loved to fucking bitch. Thank God she was obsessed with the buttery leather melting onto to her flat ass.

Syd and Ezze looked at each other. They were practically blood, after all. We'd all done it, many times before. Once, four of us crammed into one shower with only 15 minutes to get ready.

"Ron should get in first 'cause it takes forever for her to dry her hair," Ezze suggested.

"Okay, little shit. Go!" Ash shooed me off. ⚡ I took out my Sebastian No.9 and put it on the white dresser next to the metallic Aqua Net cans. Aqua Net could keep even the longest thickest hair in a stiff Mohawk…for, like, a week. But the smell of Sebastian No. 9 was heavenly. You just couldn't count on borrowing hairspray—like lipgloss—because we all used a ton. The more cans, the better.

"K. I'm going in." While I was in the shower, Ezze came in and peed.

"Are you going to be okay tonight?"

I answered with my eyes closed allowing the white foam slide down my face. "Yeah. I don't know. I guess." After my shower, I walked back into the white room and all its electricity, in my turbaned towel head and giant Fido Dido T–shirt.

The night was now ON, when we *really* got ready. ⚡

Makeup—curl lashes holding the curler at least 10 second, gently pulsating the tool. Base, concealer, shadow, eyeliner, mascara, mascara, mascara, mascara. Liner in seafoam glitter green, beginner blue, or black smudgy shit. Lips and blush. We always put a little bit of lip on before the blush. That way you knew how much blush to put on. Powder. Powder. Powder. Powder. Then panties, bras, tights or garter belts and stockings. Clothes. MORE hairspray. And more lipgloss.

Heels, boots, jewelry, fake ID, purse, and (depending on what kind of night it was) hat, bandana, and even gloves—the fingerless, the full arm leather, the short fringed fingerless leather like the ones I wanted from Leathers–n–Treasures.

There wasn't much talk when we got ready, if you can believe it. Mostly just helping each other tie or pull or brush or borrow or zip. Lots of concentration and a lot of times lots of drinks. And pot. But

NEVER NEVER before making up. Getting stoned and *then* doing your makeup was like the dumbest thing you could do, because you'd end up reapplying powder and blush so many times that you looked like a pancaked freak or that crazy homeless lady who walked around thinking she was Elizabeth Taylor. If you smoked pot, you never knew when to stop.

I scooted my new black lace Cuntempo panties with tiny red bows on over my freshly waxed triangle bit and fastened a black lace C–cup bra.

Then Syd (in her zebra–striped sweatshirt and pink mesh string bikini bottoms) and Ezze (in her wifebeater with no bra and little cotton knit coral shorts) moved over so I could use the corner of the bed closest to the outlet with all the hair tools. I had Sebastian No.9 in hand. I knew everyone wanted to use it, but they just had to wait.

Ash was still topless and applying her mascara, turning her ass to the mirror every other minute, while Syd and Ezze stared into the mirror.

I took the towel turban off my head, grabbed the blow dryer with one hand, put the Sebastian No. 9 on the floor by the bed. I lie stomach down on the bed with head hanging over the side. I was nearly upside down. But that's the best way to get big hair. All my wet ringlets hung down exposing the back of my neck. I turned the dryer on to medium–high heat, using my left hand to rake through the curls so they'd separate and followed that with hot air. ⚡ While my hair was still a little damp, I grabbed the Sebastian No. 9 and sprayed and sprayed as I ran the blow dryer from the nape of my neck down to the ends hanging just above the floor. I kept spraying different sections with the sticky fizz. Once the back of my hair was almost dry, I set everything down, and slid my body off the bed. Then I flipped my hair over, so I was fully upright again, with a perfectly huge Hesher mane.

"I hate you, bitch, " Ash teased.

"Look at you, Ronnie! The Fang is totally gonna want it tonight!" Ezze laughed sinfully. They were sweet. But I always felt I needed more help than any of them. These girls all looked amazing all the time.

I picked the Sebastian up off the ground and, with the other hand, ratted and pushed the hair on the sides of my face back by my ears, holding it in place with the tips of my fingers as I sprayed. I combed my bangs up with my fingers and whirled the can in mini–spirals just above my forehead. The key was to get everything totally BIG because by the time you got to the show, it would have calmed down. And you totally wanted it big for The Strip.

Ash's bedroom was really no different than a showgirl's dressing room at The Flamingo, with flitzy boas and bobby pins and dusting powder. I wondered if those showgirls used Aqua Net. One by one we rotated like a conveyor belt—spray, blow, down, style, up, spray—with hairspray vapor everywhere.

The girls were laughing about what might happen tonight. But I had to concentrate; I had to look HOT. I had done my own forecasting and The Fang was involved according to my hopes and dreams or fears and doubts. I didn't really know it at first, but the girls were talking about me:

She's going for it tonight!
She's bringing the babies out tonight!
She's going to lose it!

I snapped awake. "I'm not getting laid!" But the girls continued to grill me. Bras snapped, tags ripped off panties, and thigh highs were pulled up. ⚡

Sydney hardly had to make any effort—she was just naturally cute and confident because she ALWAYS had a boyfriend. And she was every boy's wet fantasy.

Ash had insane gusts of energy when getting ready for a big night that opened us up to the notion that ANYTHING could happen. And despite her incessant bitching, she really loved the mess we made.

Ezze might have looked simple in the loose black collared shirt and stretchy leggings she was pulling on, but the lace teddy underneath said it all. There might be major action for her tonight. She had a few options—Helmet or even Denny. But there was always that sadness kind of thing on her face. I didn't know if it was because she didn't like her outfit or if she could already feel the heartache she'd be dealing with tomorrow. It didn't seem fair, but it was always there, waiting to meet her in the morning.

After carefully squeezing my big hair through the neck and my arms through the long sleeves, I pulled the skintight dress down over my rump. Then I leaned forward into the mirror and adjusted the lopsided loaf at my chest. The girls began to wolf and coyote.

"I told you! She's bringing them out tonight!"

"Ron, are you going to jump his bones?"

"I don't know…" I didn't feel like it was me who was talking. It felt like someone behind me. I had done this routine so many times before and it *usually* worked out. But the mystery wouldn't detach its clampy metal teeth from the side of my brain. "I really don't know."

"Ronnie, you know that boy fucking likes you. Bitch. He fucking calls your ass, right?" Ash said, looking for her bra, even though she didn't need one.

"Yeah, but…"

"Pritchard NEVER fucking calls me. Never! I always have to fucking call him. He doesn't let me know where the parties are. And those parties The Fang tips you on always kick ass…"

"Yeah, but…"

She strapped the turquoise lace net over her mosquito bites and tossed everything on her big waterbed up and down, looking for her perfect top to wear with her perfect leather mini.

"Dude! He went to a fucking dance with you! Pritchard would NEVER go to a fucking dance with me!" Her voice was drunk loud now. "NE–VER!" She stood looking at me with her arms crossed and her boney hips cocked to one side.

"I know, but…." I said, fluffing my hair.

"Yeah, Ron," Syd applied the last bit of blush to the apples of my cheeks. "And you look hot."

Ezze was in the mirror, again, spraying her bangs. "Ron, I need your Sebastian."

I pointed to the can sitting on the nightstand behind her curvy tush. She grabbed it and popped the cap off, then fluffed her bangs up and sprayed them as they fell down. "It's the truth, babe."

"I know," I mumbled, looking down. "But…"

"Yeah," Syd started to giggle as she rummaged through her makeup. "Or else, all the other boys are going to have a boner when they see your cleavage! Damn!"

It was time to leave. I pulled out my Dior lipstick in Holiday Red and dabbed it on. "Use the Aqua Net first. It holds better," I told Ash. "Then go over it with the Sebastian so it'll smell nice."

"OK," she answered quickly. "Which shoes should I wear?" I don't know why, but it always amazed me when she asked for my advice.

"Maybe those black fringe boots," I pointed to the pair sitting at the end of her bed.

"What about these?" She held up a pair of teal snakeskin heels with diagonal cutouts at the toe.

"Black is better," I answered, but I really didn't care. ⚡

I put on my favorite party pumps with 4–inch heels and gold metal tips on the toes. I pulled out my Miss Dior perfume which smelled like sultry rose. I sprayed myself and then the girls because a major rule while traveling in a pack was to wear the same scent. Other girls made mistake of wearing a bunch of different scents. That, mixed with hairspray, was nasty, like the cheap perfume smell at the drugstore.

Everyone collected their things for the night. Then we made our way to the kitchen counter and Ash poured us each a shot of Tequila while we waited for Tess and her jungle juice drop off. And, like always, came the Tequila talk:

Which Tommy has a bigger dick?
Oh, God. She always talks about dick size.
Taylor's!
How would you know?
I heard Franco has a big Italian…
Who does he think he is? David Lee Roth?

Then I heard Tess's Camaro honking over the horny jabber.

"It's Tess!" I ran outside and met her Brownie smile.

"You're not coming in? We're doing shots."

"No. But I brought the jungle juice I made for you guys. She handed me a huge thermos and four large plastic cups with bendable straws. She had decorated them with puffy paint, everything written in hot pink, purple, and Day–Glo green. Mine read:

RAGE! RONNIE! THE FANG! LONG HAIR ROCKS! BFF! PARTY! THE INNOCENT ONE! LOVE YA! LATER, SMEGMATOR! LATER DAYS BETTER LAYS! REPULSORS! GET WASTED! MORE IS ALL YOU NEED!!! ARCADIA!

It didn't matter how many cups we had—Syd and Tess loved making them for us. We wanted to keep them forever, but it just wouldn't happen. No matter how hard we tried. It was crazy. They'd withstand a night of drunken mayhem, but get fucked up just sitting on a shelf in our room collecting dust. All because of a thing called time. ⚡

THE RIDE

I don't know how it happened.

Before I knew it, we were on the oldest freeway in LA—the snaky Dena 110 toward HOLLYWOOD. Insane speed, insane laughter inside the Big Red Bronco. We were WASTED. ⚡

It looked all foggy outside the windows, even though Los Angeles didn't really get foggy too often. But it was still the perfect temperature, when you completely forget if you're hot or cold. You just felt right. And the next day you can't stop talking about how great the weather was last night. And even though it's late, around 10 p.m., it still looks kind of light outside, and everything trails left and right.

There was no time, no fear, only faith. We simply trusted Ash and the Big Red Bronco with our lives, even when she was driving fast and looking at us (in the backseat), her long fingers wrapped around jungle juice and her pedal to the metal. Ezze handled the volume while Syd and I sang as loud as we could, relentlessly brutally jerking side to side. No matter what, we believed in her motorhead blood. Even when the thrill of the ride made her grin so wide that she looked coked up and out of her mind.

Ezze turned the volume even louder. ⚡

We banged our heads and our hair whipped fiercely as the Bronco weaved through traffic, missing collisions by mere inches. Our hearts thumped as loud as the speakers.

We were somewhere, alive and drunk beyond belief. ⚡

Even though it drove Ash crazy, I loved how we never made the light off the Freeway exit by Florentine Gardens, where the Disco Sticks stood in line. ⚡ You could see all the lazers inside whenever someone opened the door and hear Egyptian Lover boom–booming out. The Disco Sticks were their own breed who listened to the best dance music ever. While we waited for the green light, the girls passed compacts around and Ash switched her tape out, my eyes locked onto the long line waiting outside to get in that cha-cha galaxy. I was fascinated by their look and vibe. They all wore white or black or white and black. Boys had pleated pants and billowy button–up shirts with leather bolo ties, little 'staches and long eagle–like mullet waves above manicured side burns. Girls wore sticky dresses, the most scandalous hot pants, and huge doorknocker earrings that must have ripped off when they danced. They also had Lisa–Lisa–Cult–Jam banana–clipped hair with most massive chola bangs, heavy black liquid eyeliner that went from corner to corner (also chola style) and mostly hooker heels. I saw the same chonchy dresses we wore, but they decked them out with giant belts, crazy fake jewelry with huge cabochons, and cropped leather jackets. The main difference between us and them was their giant, protruding shoulder pads.

They were always there when we hit that light.

The light turned green and Ash lunged forward with that wild look in her eyes. Pritchard was close; she could just smell him. She was drunker than drunk, and hornier than life. Ezze poofed her hair and lipglossed. She looked nervous, maybe a little worried. Sydney didn't really give a fuck about the band or the boys. She just wanted to party and get drunk.

We drove past Gazzarri's, a different scene entirely from the Disco Sticks but just as good. Its huge parking lot looked like a moat around the venue. A gaggle of Mod kids packed the lot alongside rows and rows of Vespas and Lambrettas, sometimes hundreds, all Mod–ified with scores of mirrors, and raccoon tail scooter charms that hung high above the seats like flags. The more mirrors a scooter had, the cuter the boy would be, like Ace Face (or his equivalent, Ace Frehley). The boys had Davy Jones hair cuts and acrylic sweaters with racer stripes and mock turtlenecks like you'd see on old episodes of The Brady Bunch. They wore pointy "Beatle Boots" that worked well with their fitted highwater pants. And lots of olive or black parkas covered with the same Union Jack flag rockers loved with strategically placed The Who, The Jam, The Three O'Clock, The Beat, and 45 Grave patches. Sometimes they'd even have a Pandoras badge or a badge for The Seeds. The girl Mods, or Dolly Rockers, defined themselves with their hair. Bobs and long bangs smoothed out with clothing irons, a little poof at the back of their crown, and middle parts that were just slightly off center. Completely opposite from our messy tresses, but with equal amounts of ratting and Aqua Net. Even from the road, I could see their Coty–puffed powdery faces, the thick black eyeliner (that ran the same way as the Disco Sticks), and those super Mod pale lips. A lot of them wore A–line mini dresses with long onion pendants and tights in every color with very pointy flats, or rad $2 thriftstore Go–Go boots.

The Mods were a chatty muddle, always discussing what band was playing where, who broke up with whom, and where they could score beer. The Mods didn't skimp on the details. You had to go all out to be a Mod. If you half–assed it, you'd never be "in." They reminded me of photos of my mother from the '60s, especially the trippy print dresses and iron–flat hair.

I learned a little about them when I was in junior high, when the scooter gang high school would putt–putt–putt over to pick up my friend, Heidi, who was super Mod until she "fried" at a Dead show in 10th grade and never looked back.

As soon as we passed Gazzarri's, we were MINUTES away from our destination. The moment we past Gazzarri's, Alfredo's Snack Bar, and Club Lingerie, the air would literally change and for some reason everything got brighter. ⚡

I slurped the last of my jungle juice, flipped my hair over and back, and reapplied my Holiday Red lipstick. The Big Red Bronco's figurehead Ash prayed to the gods she'd get laid and an awesome parking spot.

"Fuck. I hope we get our spot," Ezze said.

"Unless some fucking bitches discovered it," Ash spat out.

I could see the mottled lights cascading onto the sidewalks down the street toward us, bouncing off all the glitter and studs and shiny shiny strands. A mile of shags, manes, helmets, rats, and Rapunzels huddled in separate puddles, connecting the dots along this notch of The Sunset Strip. ⚡

Tough Viking–esque Speed Metal men and soppy cherry–glossed boys, and all the scenes in between, underneath the flashing prism stripes of The Rainbow, a joint known for the loitering hoards outside who smoked, made out, or passed out show fliers, as well as the inebriated happenings that went on inside.

We flew to the windows like spattered bugs, quickly panning the street to see if we recognized anyone, and to check out the babes. Then, without any warning, the Big Red Bronco tilted a mean right around the corner, up the hill.

"Did you guys see anyone?" Ash asked.

"Nope." I answered. My drunken eyes sobered for a second, I think, as we slithered by all the white 1920's Spanish bungalows and perfect trees on this curvy steep street. I noticed there were no lawn jockeys here. Of course not. It was way too fucking cool here for a fucking lawn jockey. I always imagined this was where all the '70s rockstar drug orgies took place. I mean, we were just down the street from The Chateau. But those days were gone now. And we knew our favorite parking spot and this fantastic Sunset Strip scene would disappear one day, too, just like everything else we cared about.

But it was here tonight. So we took it.

The Big Red Bronco did a three–second three–point turn and took a nosedive in between a very black Cadillac and a cherry red Porsche. Ash could do this shit blindfolded. It gave her such a rush that the delicate freckles on the apples of her cheeks would pop out.

We gave each other a quick once–over, grabbed our purses, threw anything valuable, illegal, or sparkly under the seats, and leapt out and into a balancing act in 4–inch heels on a slanted street.

We shimmied our tight dresses down because they had bunched up under our asses, adjusted our panties, adjusted our boobs, sprayed our hair, and licked the front of our teeth in that cokey way. Then we made sure there weren't "any bats in the cave."

Just as I finished looking up Syd's nose, a black lacquered Ford 4x4 sped up the hill and a voice that was distinctly Devon's flew out the window with something else. "Ronnie! Grab those!"

I ran a couple hops and picked up a pair of black leather fingerless gloves with long fringe lining the outer seams. "YES!" I shouted back, waving them in the air at the truck which was making a three–point turn of its own. The girls huddled around me as I pulled them on. "She knew I really wanted these." I was stoked.

"Fuck. I have to pee," Syd informed everyone. "Ronnie, come pee with me." I peeled off the Evel Knievel gloves and handed them to Ezze, who stood there wondering if she also needed to pee. But Syd pulled me away by my elbow to a spot in a driveway near a hedge between a gold Range Rover and black Mercedes Benz parked. She just couldn't wait for Ezze.

We tiptoed toward the garage door where our jungle juice bits couldn't be seen from the road. I peeked over my shoulder. Syd had already let go a stream that was making its way down the side of the driveway and under the Rover, crossing the well–lit walkway into the pruned landscape.

"Fuck, dude," I whispered. "Hurry up. I have to pee, too." I didn't want to get caught. Syd kept giggling.

"Fucking relax. Gee–sus." She didn't care if we got caught. She could shit right there on the lawn, then pull her g–string up and walk away unscathed. She never got in trouble and, really, she'd just laugh if we ever got caught. "I'm done," she whispered. "Try not to step in my pee, dude. Or slip..."

God, I thought. *That* would be awesome; slip and fall in Syd's jungle juice piss minutes before I saw The Fang. I also didn't want to piss on myself because accidents can happen, especially if you're drunk off your ass and pissing diagonally on a slanted driveway in a dress that stuck to your body and 4–inch stilettos.

I peed as fast as possible, but my drunken pee sessions were never a couple drips.

"Fuck, dude..." Syd giggled.

"Shut up!" I laughed. I drip dried, pulled my panties up and my dress down and we scurried back to the Big Red Bronco where everyone was waiting. I jumped up and down, grabbing the gloves from Devon's hands as she waved them in my face. "Oh my God! I love them! That was so rad of you, Devon! How much??"

"No–no–no," she said waving her hand. "I didn't even pay for them," she winked.

"Oohh..." is all I said. We all turned and marched down the hill onto The Strip.

There's something injecting about The Strip, with all its whiskey fights and cars speeding by, that seeps deep inside and spreads so fast, you have zero time to think. We were pretty much the most avoided (or misunderstood) people around and we were all here together, a bunch of long hair freaks hanging out on a filthy street. And it felt like a heaven. We just hoped Ash wouldn't want to kick someone's ass.

We took a few steps and panned the crowd. It was kind of like Halloween but better, when the girls dress like sluts and the boys look like pirates. And everyone knows Halloween is lucky. ⚡

"Fucking babe!"

"He's fine as fuck!"

I didn't pay much attention to the girls I didn't know. A lot of them were just too trashy or cheap or dumb and desperate in their weird "Like–a–Virgin" outfits. But the boys—I noticed them. The idea was to hang out on the streets and be seen. So we took our time and watched them on the sidewalk littered with pink, white, and blue papers promoting bands like King Snake, Crotch, Geronimo, Mary's Lip Grip, and Suss Russ, AZAD, Chopin Cherry, and Iron Pirates, White Speed, Sugar Pussy, Crazy 8Z, Ninja Magic, Geisha Matinee, and Sweet Sweet Suicide. Most of the boys were in bands or worked with bands or wished they were in a band. ⚡

David Lee Roths and David Mustaines. Axel Rose and Michael Monroes. Sometimes we might even see the real Lemmy. Pretty boys got away with wearing tight Easter–egg colored (girls) jeans and lip gloss and bandanas with their sunray shoulder length 'dos. We'd see lots of hardcore widow lace and striped leggings with bold lines that led you right to their package. There were huge dudes, badasses in KNAC T–shirts, ripped Levi's, and a million rose, skull, or snake tattoo sleeves down their arms. There were intentional mullets, shiny lazer–cut layers, crimped poodle do's, and frizz–bo hair don'ts. Like always the hopefuls were on the outskirts, waiting patiently like a band of wusses to get IN. But they didn't get it; for the rest of us, this wasn't a choice. It just was and it was just *us*.

There were tons of longer river rat mullets and shorter stoner cuts, gypsy scarves, and cowboy bandanas. Ripped tees and no tees and leather vests with no shirts underneath, jeans with holey crotches and slit on the asses. Black and purple zebra and a lot of leopard leggings. Laced–up stretch pants and a ton of black leather pants. Pleather micro–minis and motorcycle jackets. Black veils, black stockings with the seam up the back and long fishnet "gloves." And cut-off jeans, usually worn by the drummers. Sometimes cut so short you could see their ballsack (which was gross). Cowboy boots made of python, crocodile, purple eel skin, or white leather boots with rainbow stitching. Kermit green Docs with white stitching and red combat boots with huge steel toe bumps. Fringe sleeves, fringe boots, studded gloves, spiked belts. Crosses and chains, earrings with skulls and tiny silver spoons. Silver mesh kerchief necklaces, rubber bracelets, and Hell's Angels buckles. Smudged liner and melted mascara, smeared lipstick and chipped red nail polish. And the smell of hair everywhere.

Coors Lite, Bud, Mickey's, JD. Southern Comfort, Jim Beam, Peach Schnapps or any Schnapps you stole from your parents' pantry. Boonesfarm (Strawberry Hill), vodka and orange, vodka and cranberry, and Wild Turkey. Coke, pot, angel dust and smack. I mean, you could do anything that was your heart's desire. Or you could settle for dimples and mischief and hops flavored cum. ⚡

We waited in line for a minute before I decided to head up to the bouncer with the ripped arms and Anthrax muscle–Tee that he was wearing inside out. He had the prettiest dark–walnut hair and his cherry–stained lips looked a little dry. He had last night's barely–there liner on his crystal–crystal blue eyes and his faded Levi's were almost obscene but looked hot with his fucked up Chucks.

"How long?" I asked in a very soft voice.

He smiled and touched a ringlet of hair that had fallen over my right boob.

"Who are you with, babydoll?"

"Them—" I pointed to the pack of girls. "And that boy. But he's our driver."

He laughed, "Okay," then framed a small square in the air. I smiled and motioned a cool–calm "come over" to the girls and then handed my Kodak–backed ID to the foxy doorman. He looked at it, turning it over, then handed it back with a wink. He checked the other IDs from Ezze, Syd, Ash, Devon and Dev's boyfriend, but kept looking at me. "What's your real name?" he said gently with a deep sexy voice.

I leaned in and whispered "Far–rah" in his ear. "But everyone calls me Ronnie."

"Okay." He unhooked the rope and welcomed us through the on–the–list entrance. "I'll look for you later, *Ronnie*. I'm Jack."

"Okay, *Jack*..." I walked into the damp, dank (what to me resembled) seedy boxing ring venue from back in the day. It was dark but when the spotlights hit your eyes, they were severe and WHITE. Two bars filled with filth and smoke. It reeked of cheap beer and piss and those nasty smelling Camel cigarettes. And everywhere, the thick suggestive smell of sex. I had never really done IT, but I had been around IT enough times to know what IT smelled like. ⚡

I made a beeline for the bar and nearly fell down when the Kevin Dubrow look–alike bartender caught me by the arm. He laughed and took my order. It didn't matter if I ate shit here, because there was always someone to catch me. I grabbed the first of many free drinks and plowed through the sweaty crowd. I scooted through some dudes that I called "King Supremes" because they all reminded me of comic book villains or Vikings. They had perfect hair and skullhead rings that opened up to a stash of white stuff. They were almost always into Speed Metal and could totally kick your ass if they wanted to. And you just knew they had to be HUGE. I imagined their girlfriends wore heart lockets with a picture of their boyfriend's big cock inside it.

I smelled mold and beer and hairy sweat. Cheap perfume and Aqua Net. Fried food and cigarettes. But was he here? ⚡

I pounded my drink by the time I reached the other bar at the back of the venue. I looked around and saw Ash up in front by the stage, and then I saw the rest of our Sketchwood crew.

I squeezed between two fucked up dudes who threw brawling words over my head just to get to the bartender I knew.

"Hey, cupcake," the bartender cooed.

"Hi," I flirted back. I had to. I didn't like him, but it always paid off if I was nice. And it didn't really matter to either of us. He leaned over the bar and down over me with a salivating eye that crawled quickly onto my chest. Most bartenders were pervs.

"What's your name again, cutie? Raw—Raw…"

"Raw—nie!" The music and rant amplified with every drink he shot my way. He poured and shook and poured and iced and out came something green and creamy into two shot glasses. I had no idea what the fuck it was. He pushed one in front of me and took the other for himself. "What is this?" I squinted and wrinkled my nose.

"Key lime pie…"

"What?" I said. The girls were probably wondering where I was, but I was having too much fun to care. And everything was starting to move the right way.

He shot the green cream down, slamming the empty glass on the bar, and pointing at me to "DO IT NOW!" I shot the key lime pie even though I knew I might be puking sweet—n—sour later.

"Mmmmmmm." A minute later I felt like I was in a loud tunnel. I bit my bottom lip and tilted my head a little to the right in the smoky lights, staring at the glowing halo around the bartender's head.

"Uuuuh—" I have no idea what words came out but something did and it must have made some sense because for some reason he smiled, took my hand that was anchored to the top of the bar, clammed it between his calloused fingers tattooed with tiny skulls, bent over and stole a kiss. His lips were wet and I was surprised and disappointed and then too drunk to think anymore about it. I just wanted my hand back on the counter. And God only knows where his fingers, and lips, had been.

"Hey, Smegs…" a voice behind me said as my ass was pinched.

"What's going on, Ron?" Devon chuckled. She was such a beautiful Cuban badass.

Then Syd mumbled something in Pop–Rock giggles that sounded like, "Ronnie, get us drinks from your dude."

I smiled.

"Did he try again?"

"Yeah, but it was totally gross."

"Was it wet?"

"What do you want?"

"Did you like it?"

"It was sweet and easy to get down." The girls all laughed and I protested, "The drink! The drink!"

Ash looked over the crowd and pulling her skirt down. "Just order whatever…"

Syd was so wobbly and whiny, hanging onto her purse like it was going to save her. She looked like she was about to chum, and the show hadn't even started. Ezze whispered into her ear and kept holding her up. Then she looked at me and said, "Babe, just get Cape Cods."

"OK."

"We went and said hello to the boys," Syd the drunk cheerleader started to talk. "Taylor and Rif are already out there," she slurred and pointed to the stage.

"He wasn't back there?" I asked.

"You didn't see him yet, Ron?" Ezze asked. Her gentle voice honeyed over the loudness.

The bartender pushed the Cape Cods forward with another round that was short fat thick and creamy. ⚡

I passed the shots around as little whispers shot past my ear—"HELLLL–YES!"…"Good job!"…"That's our girl."

"Free!" I replied.

Then Ash said something in a slurring Tower–of–Pisa sort of way: "Seeeee…you got two rounds of free drinks. You have nothing to worry about. Lots of dudes are hot for you…"

I stopped mid–drink and mid–confusion, my eyes rolled up off the glass rim and onto her face. What the fuck was she talking about?

"What?"

The wave of dark silhouettes poured in behind and everything started to rock diagonally—
slowly to the right
and then slowly to the left.
Slowly to the right,
and then slowly to the left.

And everything in the bar just looked darker.

"Where the fuck is Pritchard?! Fuck him! I can fuck Johnny if I want to! But I wanna fuck Pritchard…" She suspiciously rambled. But it didn't work. Even in my lush–full state of key lime pies and Cape Cods, I knew something was up. I looked around at the others. Syd was already toast. She'd be useless. Devon laughed, looking at Ash and then back at me, snorting a grunty laugh and pushing forward a very, "Ha–ha…she's just drunk and stupid" campaign. "She has no idea what the fuck she's talking about, Ron. Just ignore her and keep drinking."

I finally looked at Ezze, whose face looked serious and awake.

"Come with me," she said, pushing Syd's drunken bones onto someone else's shoulder, taking my hand, and pulling me through the raucous black sea.

"Where are we going?" She didn't answer. "EZZE! WHERE ARE WE GO–INGUH?" I asked again.

"To smoke you out…" She had her head down when the stage lights went bright and out came the band–ARCADIA.

"The boys!" I pointed back with my free arm. "They're ON!" But before I could finish, she swung me through the door to the little girl's room and positioned me in front of her and the mirrored wall. We stood there facing each other in the strangest silence as guitars railed out in the bar.

"What?" I don't know if I said it out loud but in the middle of my wobbly confusion, Ezze held both of my hands calmly in hers. ⚡

"Ronnie, don't get upset…"

"What? What!?" I said again.

"The Fang…he's here. He has his arm around a girl." With the last words, she held onto me tighter.

"WHAT?" I puffed out. At first I didn't really understand what she had said. DENIAL. DISBELIEF. My arms jerked and I felt a huge gush rushing up my throat.

"NO!" Ezze grabbed my shoulders and shook me a little. "Listen to me!" Her eyes locked onto me. "You're not going to get like that! We're going to go out there and have fun, and you're NOT going to act like you give a shit!"

I just looked at her for a minute, standing there speechless. I was frustrated. I was drunk. I wanted to scream and wail and fall. But Ezze refused REFUSED to let me.

"Okay?"

"Okay," I said with a sigh and slight headshake. I wiped away the two or three tears that broke through.

"Okay! Now fix your makeup and let's get fucked up!"

I tried to smile back, but my insides felt severed and dangling. So I wiped off the runny mascara, relined my eyes, and pinched my cheeks softly like Scarlett O'Hara.

"Ready?" Ezze said. I nodded and we walked out of the little girls' room.

The lights threw themselves at us offensively and so did the amps. When my eyes focused, I realized Ezze was facing me again. And there was The Fang, standing less than a hop away from us. But it was no use. No matter what I did or said, at that moment I felt a canyon between us. And I knew in my heart there'd be no way to reach him. ⚡

Vomit vomit vomit vomit vomit vomit vomit vomit vomit vomit
vomit vomit vomit vomit vomit vomit vomit vomit vomit vomit
vomit vomit vomit vomit vomit vomit vomit vomit vomit vomit
vomit vomit vomit vomit vomit vomit vomit vomit vomit vomit
vomit vomit vomit vomit vomit vomit vomit vomit vomit vomit
vomit vomit vomit vomit vomit vomit vomit vomit vomit vomit
vomit vomit vomit vomit vomit vomit vomit vomit vomit vomit
vomit vomit vomit vomit vomit vomit vomit vomit vomit vomit
vomit vomit vomit vomit vomit vomit vomit vomit vomit vomit
vomit vomit vomit vomit vomit vomit vomit vomit vomit vomit
vomit vomit vomit vomit vomit vomit vomit vomit vomit vomit
vomit vomit vomit vomit vomit vomit vomit vomit vomit vomit
vomit vomit vomit vomit vomit vomit vomit vomit vomit vomit
vomit vomit vomit vomit vomit vomit vomit vomit vomit vomit
vomit vomit vomit vomit vomit vomit vomit vomit vomit vomit
vomit vomit vomit vomit vomit vomit vomit vomit vomit vomit
vomit vomit vomit vomit vomit vomit vomit vomit vomit vomit
vomit vomit vomit vomit vomit vomit vomit vomit vomit vomit
vomit vomit vomit vomit vomit vomit vomit vomit vomit vomit
vomit vomit vomit vomit vomit vomit vomit vomit vomit vomit
vomit vomit vomit vomit vomit vomit vomit vomit vomit vomit
vomit vomit vomit vomit vomit vomit vomit vomit vomit vomit
vomit vomit vomit vomit vomit vomit vomit vomit vomit vomit
vomit vomit vomit vomit vomit vomit vomit vomit vomit vomit
vomit vomit vomit vomit vomit vomit vomit vomit vomit vomit
vomit vomit vomit vomit vomit vomit vomit vomit vomit vomit
vomit vomit vomit vomit vomit vomit vomit vomit vomit vomit
vomit vomit vomit vomit vomit vomit vomit vomit vomit vomit
vomit vomit vomit vomit vomit vomit vomit vomit vomit vomit
vomit vomit vomit vomit vomit vomit vomit vomit vomit vomit
vomit vomit vomit vomit vomit vomit vomit vomit vomit vomit
vomit vomit vomit vomit vomit vomit vomit vomit vomit vomit
vomit vomit vomit vomit vomit vomit vomit vomit vomit vomit
vomit vomit vomit vomit vomit vomit vomit vomit vomit vomit
vomit vomit vomit vomit vomit vomit vomit vomit vomit vomit
vomit vomit vomit vomit vomit vomit vomit vomit vomit vomit
vomit vomit vomit vomit vomit vomit vomit vomit vomit vomit
vomit vomit vomit vomit vomit vomit vomit vomit vomit vomit. Vom it.

He had been the most tender thing to me. But right now I couldn't even tilt a nervous look his way. My tongue was numb, and I was gagging on my tears. I didn't know how to feel. I didn't know how to be. All I knew was I wasn't stoned enough or drunk enough, even though I had been drinking for the last four hours. It was all very hard for me to believe.

Ezze was standing with her back to the crowd, facing me. The Fang was only two steps behind her, if that, and caught en route to the little boys' room.

Ezze was the only thing grounding me. She held my hands with a serious fix on my eyes, playing it like we were in the middle of heated girl talk. Which we were. Sort of. But I would bet anything that he knew exactly what was going on.

"Hey, Ron–nee," he said softly, playing it off in a slightly nervous manner. I wanted to think there was a some sadness on his face, and a load of guilt tucked somewhere in his words. But if he really did feel bad, it still wasn't enough for him to stop what he was doing.

"Hi," I blew out of the corner of my mouth, almost almost moving my eyes to look at him. Ezze held onto me like I was on the edge of a dinghy in a deep sea. She was not letting go, not now, no matter what happened.

"Uh, is something wrong, Ron?" This voice–I had never heard *this* voice before. This baby sweetie koochie–koo bullshit voice. Now I knew it was serious. I knew it was true.

"NO–THING is wrong…" Ezze batted back with an eyebrow up. Never letting go of me.

"Oooh–kaay," The Fang belted an awkward chuckle and walked three steps into the little boys' room.

Ezze shook her head and mumbled, "What a dick."

I felt a stranger. In a world that had been mine.

It was fucked. My chest went concave and I could feel the pressure rise until it was under my chin, right where it touches the top part of your neck and makes you gag. The heaviness of tonight slipped back into my eyes and fell like boulders down through my veins.

I hadn't asked for it. Or had I? Well, I hadn't chased him. He had squawked and squawked and done jumping jacks in front of me until I stopped and "looked" at him. And every time I looked, I liked what I saw. I liked what I felt. And I let him in. But now I realized the game, how he'd only take me so far and then push me back into square on again. No. I didn't think this was fair. But I guess anything I thought didn't fucking matter. Here I was, a half–dead guppy caught on his line, getting dragged around his shallow insides…

slowly…
to the left…
slowly…
to the right…

…until I was so dumbed down and nearly blind. Because every time I'd see him, he'd somehow redeem himself with those sweet laughs and amazing dimples and all that stuff makes you just give up on the rules because it just feels right.

I knew about all these fucking rules, but no one ever taught me what real love was. I mean if it was pounding me in the face, I'd never know. I only knew how to gage shit like love with "REAL" things, crap like The Fang calling me. The Fang holding my hand. The Fang looking at me. But it wasn't really the "looking." It's what was happening in the space between his look and mine. No one ever fucking explained that shit to me. What did it fucking mean? To toggle back and forth between *that* reality and *this* feeling made me want to vomit, lock up, and shut down.

Was *anything* in this world real?

I stood still, with my claws deeply pressed into my flesh, until I had secured a hard anchor. As I started to tear my meaty center open, Ezze gripped my hands tighter.

"Hey! Wake up! Come back!" she said with a little shake, "Let's go have a good time."

I managed to nod, with the vomit still lodged in my throat. What else could I do but follow her?

A couple minutes later we were in front of the stage, singing ArcadiA and hooting with our hands high in the air. At least I think I was. All I knew was to look straight ahead. Ezze was on one side of me and Syd was on the other, with their arms on my shoulders and around my waist. Ash stood tall between me and the crowd behind us. Devon and Taylor were on each side of her. A quick glimpse from the corner of my eye found The Fang looking down at a girl I recognized because she worked as a waitress for my father! I couldn't fucking believe it. I was sickened and shocked, but I didn't dare show it.

How could he not see me? ⚡

Vomit vomit vomit vomit vomit vomit vomit vomit vomit vomit
vomit vomit vomit vomit vomit vomit vomit vomit vomit vomit
vomit vomit vomit vomit vomit vomit vomit vomit vomit vomit
vomit vomit vomit vomit vomit vomit vomit vomit vomit vomit
vomit vomit vomit vomit vomit vomit vomit vomit vomit VOMIT
vomit vomit vomit vomit vomit vomit vomit vomit vomit vomit
vomit vomit vomit vomit vomit vomit vomit vomit vomit vomit
vomit vomit vomit vomit vomit vomit vomit vomit vomit vomit
vomit vomit vomit vomit vomit vomit vomit vomit vomit vomit
vomit vomit vomit vomit vomit vomit vomit vomit vomit vomit
vomit vomit vomit vomit vomit vomit vomit vomit vomit vomit
vomit vomit vomit vomit vomit vomit vomit vomit vomit vomit
vomit vomit vomit vomit vomit vomit vomit vomit vomit vomit
vomit vomit vomit vomit vomit vomit vomit vomit vomit vomit
vomit vomit vomit vomit vomit vomit vomit vomit vomit vomit
vomit vomit vomit vomit vomit vomit vomit vomit vomit vomit
vomit vomit vomit vomit vomit vomit vomit vomit vomit vomit
vomit vomit vomit vomit vomit vomit vomit vomit vomit vomit
vomit vomit vomit vomit vomit vomit vomit vomit vomit VOMIT
vomit vomit vomit vomit vomit vomit vomit vomit vomit vomit
vomit vomit vomit vomit vomit vomit vomit vomit vomit vomit
vomit vomit vomit vomit vomit vomit vomit vomit vomit vomit
vomit vomit vomit vomit vomit vomit vomit vomit vomit vomit
vomit vomit vomit vomit vomit vomit vomit vomit vomit vomit
vomit vomit vomit vomit vomit vomit vomit vomit vomit vomit
vomit vomit vomit vomit vomit vomit vomit vomit vomit vomit
vomit vomit vomit vomit vomit vomit vomit vomit vomit vomit
vomit vomit vomit vomit vomit vomit vomit vomit vomit vomit
vomit vomit vomit vomit vomit vomit vomit vomit vomit vomit
vomit vomit vomit vomit vomit vomit vomit vomit vomit vomit
vomit vomit vomit vomit vomit vomit vomit vomit vomit vomit
vomit vomit vomit vomit vomit vomit vomit vomit vomit vomit
vomit vomit vomit vomit vomit vomit vomit vomit vomit vomit
vomit vomit vomit vomit vomit vomit vomit vomit vomit vomit
vomit vomit vomit vomit vomit vomit vomit vomit vomit vomit
vomit vomit vomit vomit vomit vomit vomit vomit vomit vomit
vomit vomit vomit vomit vomit vomit vomit vomit vomit vomit
vomit vomit vomit vomit vomit vomit vomit vomit vomit. VOMIT.

I felt the girls tighten up around me, and they played it off like none of us cared. ⚡

I woke up with my sweaty cheek stuck to the wonderfully cold bathtub rim. I couldn't remember leaving, or going to the afterparty, or maybe I could. I think I had doubled everything that poured in my mouth and I think some surferish blond dude kept making fun of how I flip my hair. "Should I wear it on THIS side or THIS side?" he had mocked with a toy doll voice. I couldn't remember getting home. Fuck. *Why was I home?* God, I needed Lita today. Lita was comforting and consistent, accessible and delicious.

Why couldn't everything be like Lita?

Then the locked door handle shook.

"Far–rah! What are you doing in there? You better be here when I get home from work tonight!" ⚡

Vomit vomit vomit vomit vomit vomit vomit vomit vomit vomit
vomit vomit vomit vomit vomit vomit vomit vomit vomit vomit
vomit vomit vomit vomit vomit vomit vomit vomit vomit vomit
vomit vomit vomit vomit vomit vomit vomit vomit vomit vomit
vomit vomit vomit vomit vomit vomit vomit vomit vomit vomit
vomit vomit vomit vomit vomit vomit vomit vomit vomit vomit
vomit vomit vomit vomit vomit vomit vomit vomit vomit vomit
vomit vomit vomit vomit vomit vomit vomit vomit vomit vomit
vomit vomit vomit vomit vomit vomit vomit vomit vomit vomit
vomit vomit vomit vomit vomit vomit vomit vomit vomit vomit
vomit vomit vomit vomit vomit vomit vomit vomit vomit vomit
vomit vomit vomit vomit vomit vomit vomit vomit vomit vomit
vomit vomit vomit vomit vomit vomit vomit vomit vomit vomit
vomit vomit vomit vomit vomit vomit vomit vomit vomit vomit
vomit vomit vomit vomit vomit vomit vomit vomit vomit vomit
vomit vomit vomit vomit vomit vomit vomit vomit vomit vomit
vomit vomit vomit vomit vomit vomit vomit vomit vomit vomit
vomit vomit vomit vomit vomit vomit vomit vomit vomit vomit
vomit vomit vomit vomit vomit vomit vomit vomit vomit vomit
vomit vomit vomit vomit vomit vomit vomit vomit vomit vomit
vomit vomit vomit vomit vomit vomit vomit vomit vomit vomit
vomit vomit vomit vomit vomit vomit vomit vomit vomit vomit
vomit vomit vomit vomit vomit vomit vomit vomit vomit vomit
vomit vomit vomit vomit vomit vomit vomit vomit vomit vomit
vomit vomit vomit vomit vomit vomit vomit vomit vomit vomit
vomit vomit vomit vomit vomit vomit vomit vomit vomit vomit
vomit vomit vomit vomit vomit vomit vomit vomit vomit vomit
vomit vomit vomit vomit vomit vomit vomit vomit vomit vomit
vomit vomit vomit vomit vomit vomit vomit vomit vomit vomit
vomit vomit vomit vomit vomit vomit vomit vomit vomit vomit
vomit vomit vomit vomit vomit vomit vomit vomit vomit vomit
vomit vomit vomit vomit vomit vomit vomit vomit vomit vomit
vomit vomit vomit vomit vomit vomit vomit vomit vomit vomit
vomit vomit vomit vomit vomit vomit vomit vomit vomit vomit
vomit vomit vomit vomit vomit vomit vomit vomit vomit vomit
vomit vomit vomit vomit vomit vomit vomit vomit vomit vomit
vomit vomit vomit vomit vomit vomit vomit vomit vomit vomit
vomit vomit vomit vomit vomit vomit vomit vomit vomit vomit
vomit vomit vomit vomit vomit vomit vomit vomit vomit vomit
vomit vomit vomit vomit vomit vomit vomit vomit vomit vomit
vomit vomit vomit vomit vomit vomit vomit vomit vomit. VOMIT.

LATER, SMEGMATOR

Six–string black bikini with Rio cut bottoms. Six–string royal blue bikini with citrus yellow strings and all–over puffy lemon–lime fish. Six–string white bikini with French–cut v–dip bottoms. Rio cut in back, of course. Black foam flip flops. Van Halen 1984 T–shirt. Ratt T–shirt. AC/DC T–shirt. Grateful Dead T–shirt. Micro–mini denim shorts with faux skirt front (sailor–ish). White denim hot pants with all–over butterfly print in brick red, sky blue, and brown. Cotton thong panties. Satin g–strings. Red lace, black lace string bikini panties. White stiletto pumps. Black leggings. Tank tops in black, white, and striped black and red. Giant poolside T–shirt with hot pink and black paint splashes. Repulsors T–shirt. Homemade Sharpie ArcadiA T–shirt. Plastic green visor from Vegas. Mirrored cop aviators. Gargoyles. Ray–Ban Baloramas. White stretch pants with mini black polka dots. Hawaiian Tropics pure banana oil. Bain de Soleil face block. Point–n–shoot camera. 35mm film. Notebooks. Pens. Black, pink, teal, striped, and dotted beach towel.

Everything was laid out on my parents' bed.

I stuffed the big duffle bag I had pulled out of their walk–in closet. In only three hours, we'd be south of Rosarito, getting wasted on Bohemia and tequila shots, rolling around drunk at Señor Fish, avoiding flying puke from the frat party upstairs, and feasting on lobster, stretchy tortillas, and the best 25–cent fish tacos, Baja style, made by some rad surfer's wife in a little side shack. And I'd venture off with Devon to a cardboard box *mariscos* stand on the side of dirt road, where she felt "they make it best." It being giant clam cocktails with Mexican seasoning and sweet tomato sauce poured out of an old plastic ketchup bottle, all served up with crackers from an old lettuce crate.

Hea—ven.

I used all my strength to force everything into the duffle. Ash would be here soon, and I had to be ready. Then my mom's cordless phone rang.

"Hello?"

"Hey—ey—ey." The voice on the other end was nervous and cute and terribly familiar. And terribly surprising. It had been over a month, maybe more, of absolutely nothing.

"Uh, hi…"

"What are you doing, Ron—neeee?"

"Packing." I was stiff. My left hand up to my head and my right going over vacation necessities again as I stood over the queen—sized Pretty-in—Pink bed with white, pink, and black Anastasia sheets.

"Oooh…packing. Pack—ing? For what?"

"For whatever," I said. "Why are you calling?"

"Uh…" His voice sounded a little scared. Or something. Sort of the same as it was at the show the last time I had seen him. But his attention was totally on me now. And I remembered my dad telling me that the girl he was with that night had cried at work, and he had overheard her repeating something like, "I thought he really liked me." But at the time I didn't understand."Um, did you get the pictures from the dance back?"

"You want to know if I got the pictures from the dance back?"

"Yeah…"

"Yeah, I got them back a while ago. Why?"

"*Why?*"

"Yeah, why?"

"Uh...because I want to see them..." He sounded a little snotty.

"You want to see them? *Really?*"

"*Really...*"

"Well, I'm leaving. And you're 21. Why would you want pictures from a high school dance?"

"Be–CAUSE..."

"*Be–cause?*"

"Be–cause, be–cause I want to see the pictures from the dance, okay?"

"Well—how? How are you going to see the dance pictures? Are you going to come get them?"

"Uh, noooo...."

"Well, how are you going to see them then? And I still don't get why you'd even want them or why you care? Why would a 21 year old want pictures from a high school dance?"

"Well, I do. I went to the dance with you and I want to see them."

"Yeah, right. That's not why you're calling..." I mumbled, teeth–on–teeth.

"What?"

"Nothing. I didn't say anything..."

"Yeah you did. I heard you…"

"Whatever. You never hear *anything*."

"Yes I do! You know that's bull–shit!"

"Yep," I mumbled again.

"Ron, what the hell is wrong with you? You're never like this! It's not like you were my girlfriend…"

Quietly I said, "You're right…"

Then his voice got sugary. Like saccharin.

"Ron…come on…"

"Open your eyes…"

"What?"

"Just for once open your eyes…"

The pause as I stood with the plastic phone in hand, eyeing the paste–y condo walls. I looked into my palm, at all the notes, at all the lines. Everything I needed was now a perspired smudge. Except for a couple of letters I could barely make out…T R U…

Then the honk–honk–honk of Ash's Big Red Bronco called.

THIS is all you need. ⚡

THE FUCKING END

SOUNDTRACK

SOUNDTRACK

SOUNDTRACK

"arcadia" Dictionary.com. Web. 2012

Thoreau, Henry David, *Walden, 18. Conclusion.*

Barrett Browning, Elizabeth, *How Do I Love Thee?*

ACKNOWLEDGEMENTS

Special thanks and love to PJ Mark (the most amazing agent/supporter ev-er…and friend), Bunny, my amazing gorgeous grandmother (Azeezjoon), Clare Sabatini and Azad Sadjadi (plus the other rad PDX kids: Nikki, Matt, Chad, Joel, Julien, Lara), Monica and Frank Percic, Walter Cessna, Bardi Johannsson, Chris Lewless, Masayo Kishi, Brianna Ragel, Tofer Chin, Chantelle Patterson, Chris Matty. D.W. Frydendahl, Michael J. Ready, Guy Ready, Ryan Ready, Drew Ready, Marc Pebley, the deKarrs, Grandmother and Poppa, Christopher Bettig, Robin Rosenberg and Lauren Ranke and all the kids at W+K, Chris Grenness, Kelly Tunstall, Heidi Hartwig, S.K. AKA Bigfoot, Amy Davis and Jon Moritsugu, Adam Glickman, Lee Taylor (from *Flux* magazine in the UK), Dustin Beatty, Scott Andrew Snyder, Joe Schweitzer, Chris Yormick, Lisa Longo, Mike "Digger" Durgerian, Spidey de Montrond, Tmoe, Adele Mildred Pederson, Paul Marlow, Brian Ermanski, Deana Bianco, John "JTMR" Reeves, Joey Gu, Liz Baca, Willow O'Brien, Peggi Jeung, Neal Hevel, Margo Silver, Maybeparade, PDX, NYC, LA, Taco Lita, Del Taco, Magnolia Bakery, doughnut makers, my elementary school teachers who championed my talents, my English and journalism teachers who understood where I was coming from and told me to keep moving with it, my editors and the copy/sub editors who sent amazing messages that kept my head up, Miss Hannah, Mrs. Tuttle, Mrs. (Mikki) Bolliger, the great John Burks of Rolling Stone, the Authors League Fund and Change Inc (they support writers!), all the friends who fed me, the surfers and rockers who I'm still close to and receive support from to this day, the writers who inspired me (HST, HM, EEC, SP, PH, JC, JK, JS, FSF and the great JDS), David Lee Roth, every Heavy Metal (and Punk Rock) band I listened to growing up. This is my love letter to the genre and to the players of the Sunset Strip.x

MANDANA TOWHIDY is a writer, editor, and art director whose work has been featured in pop culture magazines *Dazed&Confused*, *Tokion*, *Oyster*, and numerous other print and online publications. Mandana lived in Arizona as a child before moving to Los Angeles in the '80s where she was mystified by fashion and music scenes in the city (even though she was too young to actually experience them). She writes daily with her little Chihuahua, Lotte, sleeping by her side.

Made in the USA
Lexington, KY
30 July 2017